# Clarissa Maine

## The Maiden of Jilrir

David Parker Ross

First Edition 2026

# Contents

# Authors Note

As a tale set in the world of the House of Maine, one may have assumptions about its relationship to that series. It is set 100 years before the events affecting Rachael, Breanna, and Petra and may be considered a prequel, yet only the bloodline and locations are connected.

It stands alone as a trilogy.

# Chapter One

## A Girl Called Clarissa

There was much merriment in the Fatted Calf Inn that late winter evening. Whilst not the most salubrious of places, it was a popular haunt of the lower-class residents of the surrounding tenement district of the City of Jilrir.

The thick smoke of tobacco and other plant-based substances filled the air. Kevin Kurdow, the innkeeper's son, was doing a jig on one of the tables whilst the drunken crowd around him cheered him on and applauded as the fiddler played. Even Clarissa clapped along as she sat back with her chair tipped back against the wall and her boots up on the table, crossed at the ankles. She only stood out from the rest of the crowd by two things. Her high-quality tan riding britches with matching ankle boots and a waistcoat over a puff-sleeved shirt were cut above the usual dress of the denizens of this part of the city. Her wide-brimmed felt hat was pulled low over her face to conceal her identity and avoid recognition. Not that anyone would recognize her in this part of town, but why take chances? The other factor that was quite outstanding about her was that she was a woman. Not that women did not frequent the Fatted Calf. On the contrary, about a third of the people around her were female. No, what stood out about her was that she was neither a barmaid nor a whore. Although her virtue did not quite meet her family's expectations, she had some limitations and those around her, unaware of her true identity, did not judge her by the same standards. Most knew her as just Clarissa. She was obviously a woman of some means, for she often bought others drinks, and clearly a fun-loving girl, for she would frequently be amongst the merrymakers dancing and singing.

"Clarissa!" Kevin Kurdow called to her over the noise and grinned down at her, beckoning for her to come up and join him. She chuckled and shook her head, dismissing him with a wave of her hand and raising her glass to indicate she was enjoying her drink. She liked the short, cheerful man who clearly had eyes for her. She had often pondered taking the man with his rough working-class hands to bed, but something always stopped her. She *really* liked him. It may ruin that bond of friendship if she were to cross that line. It was bad enough that their relationship was based on a lie.

"Oh, come on, come on," he shouted with a mock imploring expression. He reached out a hand to her despite the fact that she was far out of his reach. This led some of the revelers to turn to the girl who sat quietly, cheering her on to join the merriment. She gave in and downed her whisky in one go, wiped her lips with the back of her hand, pulled her feet off the table, and stood up, grabbing Kurdow's hand. He helped her up onto the table and slipped her arm in his. She joined in the fast-moving jig as the fiddler sped up his jaunt. She glared down at him in both a chastising and yet amused manner. She continued with Kurdow for several dances, moving around the table, switching arms, kicking up her legs, and generally having a good time until the fiddler himself needed to take a rest. She kissed Kurdow on the cheek and then jumped back down, returning to a table where her friend Maddie was now sitting. The increase in both her years and girth had significantly decreased her value as a lady of the night. She was still attractive, but not a patch on those girls ten years younger than her, still in their twenties.

"I don't know how you have the energy, my dear." Maddie chuckled, handing her the drink that she had ordered.

Clarissa flopped down in the seat beside her with a grin. "Oh, I don't know, Maddie, I'm quite sure when you spread your legs for the punters you're using a lot more energy than I do."

Maddie chuckled. "Oh, I just lie back and think of Jilrir mostly." Her smile turned to a smirk as she continued. "You know, with a figure like yours and a face like that, you could make at least ten or fifteen Sivs a night. We could start you out with the tamer punters."

"Maybe so." Clarissa grinned. "But I am quite content to live by my current means."

Maddie smirked and tilted her head slightly. "You know you're not as mysterious as you think you are, Clarissa."

Clarissa tilted her head back at her. "I'm not trying to be mysterious at all, Maddie. Whatever could you be thinking of?" She sounded innocent.

"We hear it in your voice, my dear," Maddie said knowingly. "You struggle to hide it when you've had a few drinks."

"I have no idea what you mean, my dear Maddie." But as she said it, she looked around the room to avoid the gaze of her friend.

"You try to sound like us, but when you're a little bit tipsy, you get all posh." Maddie narrowed her eyes, but her smile did not dissipate.

"Maybe that's just the effect of the drink," Clarissa replied, downing the whiskey in one go and then waving to the barmaid for another with two fingers, indicating an additional one for her companion.

"Then tell me what it is you do." Maddie now sounded frustrated, for she always liked to be in other people's business. "Your purse is nearly always full, and some of us would like to get in on a little bit of that action."

Clarissa kicked her chair back again, leaning against the wall. Her mind raced for a response while she struggled to maintain a casual air. "Oh, I assure you, Maddie, there's no action to get in on. My business partners are not looking to expand their operations."

"Come on, tell me what it is?" Maddie squeezed her knee affectionately. "Smuggling? Racketeering? It's gotta be something illegal for you to be such a mystery all the time."

Clarissa turned to face her with a hard stare. "It is the sort of business you should keep your nose out of. Were I to tell it, my partners would cut my throat and leave my body out for the buzzards."

Maddie almost paled under the intensity of the look. "Are we talking The Tallymen here?"

"Yes, Maddie. We are talking The Tallymen here," replied Clarissa ominously, having no idea what this 'Tallymen' was.

"Understood, Clarissa. I will say no more about it," Maddie replied nervously. She looked over at the bar where young Kevin Kurdow was studying them with keen interest. "Are you ever going to put that boy out of his misery?"

Clarissa followed Maddie's gaze, and when her eyes met Kevin's, "Oh, again, I have no idea what you mean, Maddie," she said with a sappy, amused grin.

"Stuff and nonsense!" Maddie snorted. "That boy goes to bed wondering what it would be like to get between your thighs, and from that stupid grin on your face, you would clearly welcome him in."

Clarissa frowned and tilted her head at her friend. "Must you always be quite so crude, Maddie? Is there not a romantic bone in your body?"

Maddie gave a little harrumph and folded her arms. "Romance is for idiots and little girls, not men and women. You could do worse than Kevin Kurdow, you know. He stands to inherit the tenancy of this inn. A permanent roof over your head and a nice little earner."

Clarissa let out a sigh. "Kevin is absolutely adorable, but unfortunately, we are worlds apart. It would be too dangerous to bring him into my life. No, he needs to find himself a quiet, unassuming wife who will take care of him and help him run the inn."

"Doesn't the quiet life appeal to you?" Maddie chuckled. "Kevin can give you security. He's a handsome lad, and he's a well-endowed and tender lover."

Clarissa spun round at her, her face grim. "You have lain with him?" She said, her eyes widening in surprise.

"Do you think we girls get to use the facilities here for free?" Maddie chuckled.

"Honestly, I didn't think he was the sort of person to pay for it," Clarissa said, blushing slightly.

Maddie laughed loudly. "He's a man, Clarissa. Men have their needs, and most of those needs involve food and ale in their bellies or wetting their cock."

The young woman shook her head, chuckling. "I love you, Maddie, but you have an appalling way of putting things."

Before Maddie could say anything else, a silence started to fall around the room until no one spoke. They both looked about to see what was going on. Clarissa gasped as she saw the two grim officers from the Palace Guard coming in the front door. Whilst it was obviously never unheard of for the military to go into an inn, the Fatted Calf was not exactly the sort of place the high-ranking elite of Baron Maine's entourage would have visited, especially dressed in their outlandish red and gold uniforms. No, if they were here, they meant business. They started looking around the room, and to Maddie's surprise, Clarissa suddenly scrabbled to get down under the table.

"Darling, they're not looking for you, girl." Maddie bent down and whispered hastily to the girl who was looking for the best way to get to the back exit without being noticed.

"Oh, I'm fairly confident they *are* looking for me, Maddie," she hissed back. "If you care about me at all, please do something to distract them."

Maddie gave her single nod and, steeling herself, she jumped up out of her seat and put on her beaming, come fuck me smile and strode over to them, swinging her hips. "Gentlemen, what be your pleasure? A whiskey to tickle your throat or maybe one of the girls to tickle something else?"

"Stand aside, whore," he demanded contemptuously, and she complied, for as much as she may have liked Clarissa, she was not going to spend a night in the lockup for her.

The senior of the two men stepped towards the centre of the room. "We are looking for a girl. She is so high." He put out a hand, giving a brief approximation of Clarissa's height. "Golden hair that comes down around her shoulders." The gold matched Clarissa's description, but her hair was currently tied into a very tight plait, which hung over her shoulder. "She has a small scar on the back of her right hand." Instinctively, Clarissa favoured the small scar with her left hand as she looked about the room, hoping to find an escape. Once more, her eyes met those of Kevin, who was looking at her with confusion. He looked over at Maddie, then at the barmaid standing near her carrying a tray of beer, and he nodded. Maddie got the message, and with the officers' backs to her, she swung her hand up under the tray, knocking it from the barmaid's hands. Beer spilled everywhere, and the clatter of the tray and mugs hitting the straw-covered floor made everyone in the room turn around.

Kevin beckoned Clarissa to come towards him as he headed towards the back door. She wasted no time scampering between the legs of the punters who bore no love for authority and were not likely to sell her out unless a reward was offered. Breathlessly, she made it to the bar area and slipped behind it, sitting back on the other side and out of sight.

Kevin gently tapped the back door open with his foot, and he followed the fugitive into the backroom as she scampered on her hands and knees, shutting the door behind him. They could hear the officers talking on the other side, but couldn't make out the words. Kevin pulled Clarissa up by the hand. "Thank you," she said, but he just smiled at her. Still holding her hand, he led her out to the back door and towards the stables.

However, she had no time to saddle and mount a horse as they heard the inner door open once more. She quickly squeezed Kevin's hand and let go. She ran around to the back of the stables as the two guards came out.

"She went that way," she heard Kevin shout, knowing full well he would be indicating the wrong direction.

She swiftly climbed over the fence and ran down Perch Street and up the back alleys and out into Church Street, passing the Marran temple that had been converted from one of the terraced houses and was covered in the ivy greenery of the Goddess of Nature.

The twin moons lit her way, with her thinking this was both a curse and a blessing as she crossed a little greenery at the centre of Church Street. She could avoid tripping on the shrubbery, but she would also be clearly seen. She began to slow down, thinking she had lost the pursuers. However, the breeze turned back in her direction, and she could hear their voices getting closer.

She came out by the residence of the provincial baron, Azrael Maine. The Great House sat at the centre of the city. Palace guards manned the walls, so she avoided the front entrance, moving around to the back, where there was a smaller gate, and she slipped in unnoticed. She trotted across the grass of the well-maintained lawn, reached the rose trellis, and began to climb. When she reached the second floor, she opened the window that she knew to be unlatched and climbed inside.

However, just as she was closing and latching the window, the door to the room opened, and the woman who entered let out a scream upon seeing the dark figure silhouetted in the moonlight.

"Shut up, shut up, Emily," Clarissa said in a loud whisper to Emily, her lady-in-waiting. "It's only me."

"Well, mercy me, my Lady Clarissa, you are surely going to give an old lady a heart attack," She replied, dramatically clutching at her heart. "What are you up to now, milady?"

"That doesn't matter," Clarissa said as she crossed the room, struck a match, and lit a small lantern. "What does my father know of my absence?"

"He came to see you and found you weren't in your room, and suspected that you had left without his leave again." The old lady stepped further into the room.

"How did he know where to send the guards?" Clarissa growled. The lady in waiting blushed, giving Clarissa an answer. "You betrayed me. After all our years together?" She said, her tone a mixture of anger and disappointment.

"Forgive me, my lady, but to be fair, the baron was in such a temper, and I was so afraid."

Clarissa sighed. She could not remain angry at the only lady who had mostly raised her, and she knew her father's temper, and indeed it was most ferocious and intimidating. "Do not worry, but can I trust you to cover for me now?"

"I'll do whatever I can, my lady," Emily said unconvincingly.

"Fine, go tell my father that you found me in bed."

"But he knows you weren't here!"

"Let me worry about that," said Clarissa impatiently. "Just go tell him while I change."

The old lady hurried out as Clarissa began to strip off her outfit and hid it under her bed in a little drawer on wheels. She then pulled on a nightshirt, untied her hair from its braid, and climbed into the large four-poster bed, pulling the blankets up over her. She waited as minutes passed, and then the door opened, not at all gently.

"Get up, Clarissa." Her father shouted. He was a tall, gaunt man with sunken cheeks, an overly large nose, and piercing brown eyes.

She sat up quickly, trying to look as though he had just woken her up. "Daddy, what in The Land is the matter?" She said, trying to sound a mix of shocked and sleepy.

"You went out of this house again without my permission, and from my understanding, you went to a house of ill repute."

The Fatted Calf was hardly a house of ill repute, at least not for the most part, but she couldn't exactly argue that and feign ignorance. "I assure you, Daddy, I never left the house, and I have been here in my room for several hours. Ever since dinner, in fact." She paused, pretending to ponder. "Well, apart from the time when I went down to the kitchens to get some water."

Her father stopped in his tracks about a foot from her bed and frowned. "Why would you go get yourself some water and not ring the bell for service?"

Clarissa sighed. "Oh, Daddy, Emily is getting so old now, and she really does need her sleep. I just didn't want to bother her."

"Servants are here to wait on you, not the other way around, Clarissa." Her father snapped back. "There should be no reason for you to go into the kitchens."

"The important thing is that I am safe here at home, and you have nothing to worry about. I just wish you trusted me!" She said, her voice that of hurt innocence.

"You have given me no reason to trust you, Clarissa. You have snuck out of the Great House many times." He waved his hand dismissively.

"Considering the thrashing you gave me the last time you caught me, I'm certainly not going to risk that again." She glared at him.

The baron flushed slightly. "Yes, well, I'm sorry about that," he said awkwardly. "I shouldn't have done that, but as it has apparently taught you your lesson, maybe it was appropriate after all."

"You worry too much, Daddy." She slipped out of bed and trotted up to him, ignoring the cold of the marble floor on her bare feet. Standing on her tiptoes gave him the biggest hug. She felt the tension leave his body as he relaxed, and she knew she had gotten away with it. After a moment, he returned the hug.

"You know I'm just concerned about your safety, my dear," he said in soft, fatherly tones.

"I know, Daddy, and I love you for it." She hugged him again.

"Go on, go back to bed. Tomorrow is going to be a big day, for your fiancé arrives in the morning."

"I know it's exciting, isn't it, Daddy?" She said overexcitedly. "I haven't seen him since we were betrothed when I was three."

Her father narrowed his eyes. "Knock off the sarcasm, Clarissa. You should feel privileged. Your fiancé is the Crown Prince of The Land, which means one day you will be the queen."

Clarissa pouted. "But it means I'll have to leave you, daddy, and move to Aranar, and that really is my only problem with the situation." She lied.

Her father grinned and slowly shook his head. "You may be able to wrap me round your little finger, my daughter, but that doesn't mean I'm too stupid to realise when you are kissing up to me. Goodnight, Clarissa." He kissed her on the forehead and, turning, headed out the door, closing it behind him.

The golden smile that she had offered her father instantly dissipated as she flumped back down onto the edge of the bed. She bit her thumbnail, as she often did when stressed. That had been a close call, but it was nothing to the impending meeting with Prince Campion, who was coming to claim her.

She fell back on the bed with her legs still hanging off the edge and stared up at the ornately carved canopy above her. Life as a Lady of Jilrir was intensely boring, and the idea of becoming queen of all The Land was even more abhorrent. She wanted to live the fantasy life that she had convinced the patrons of the Fatted Calf she led. For while there were suspicions that she was a cut above them, no one knew that she was the Second Lady of Jilrir, daughter of the Baron Maine. For most of her life, she had snuck out of the Great House and explored the city in the dead of night. She desperately sought the open road, adventure, and a little bit of chaos... but now, all that was coming to an end. As the King's consort, she would be watched day and night, and she fervently wished this were a destiny she could escape.

# CHAPTER TWO

# *The Crown Prince*

The Great House at the center of Jilrir was considerably humble in comparison to the estates of the barons of the other provinces. Built two hundred years earlier by Harcourt Maine, the first Maine to rule the region, it was only three stories tall. It bore only fifteen staterooms and one grand hall, which doubled as both a ballroom and a dining room depending upon the occasion. The walled city had been constructed in a time history had forgotten, when others ruled The Land. Technically, all land was the property of the king, but he resided far away in the Province of Aranar. The House of Maine considered it theirs and managed the province with impunity.

Azriel Maine was in his fifties when he ascended to the office of baron, and his primary duty was to prepare his son to succeed him. Clarence Maine was approximately six minutes older than his twin sister Clarissa, not that that would have mattered, for even if she had been born first, the title always went to the oldest male heir.

Growing up, almost all the attention focused on Clarence. He received the finest education. He was trained to lead the military. As young as fourteen, he was given responsibilities within the government. On the other hand, Clarissa was taught to sew. A pointless task considering she would never actually need to sew anything, as it was hardly like the Maines would make do and mend or create their own clothing. She was taught the social graces of being a lady, including the proper way to curtsy, sit, and hold a knife and fork, but mostly to look pretty and shut up.

There was no doubt that Clarissa Maine was attractive. The Maine men chose their wives on looks and grace rather than wit and intelligence. Not that her mother was stupid, far from it. It was simply that intellect was a bonus rather than a requirement.

Whilst Clarissa remained close to her brother — a bond she valued throughout her life — she grew more distant from her parents, especially her father, as time passed. His expectations of her were set in the tradition and values of the patriarchal system. She had one purpose in existing ... a marriage that would raise the House of Maine's profile. Azrael, being a close friend of the king, was absolutely delighted when it was suggested that his daughter be betrothed to Crown Prince Campion when she was only three years old, and he jumped at the opportunity. Ithia was one of the smaller provinces, and outside of the City of Jilrir, it was predominantly an agricultural region. In many ways, the House of Maine was considered one of the lesser houses. The union would place the Maines within the Line of Kings, a position of the highest prestige and power. Azrael would become the father-in-law of the future king and the grandfather of his issue.

The intent was that Clarissa would marry Campion when she had her first blood, but there had been a falling out between the king and the Lord of Jilrir. It took seven long years for that rift to heal before, finally, the king forgave Azrael for whatever slight had offended him. Now, with Clarissa at nineteen, the plans for the union were to go ahead.

The baron didn't really have a concept of Clarissa's opinion on the matter. He knew that she wasn't overly excited about the idea of moving to the capitol, Aranar, but he had no concept that she found the idea completely and utterly contemptible. Clarissa had not, until recently, ever considered going against her parents' wishes, for she was raised to believe that was the way and that was the expectation.

The morning after her near capture, sneaking out to the Fatted Calf, Clarissa was woken early in order to prepare for Prince Campion's arrival. She had a dull hangover from the amount of whiskey she had consumed, which didn't improve her mood about the coming events. Emily and two other servants arrived to help her dress in the large, flowery, frilly dress her father had selected for her. However, it was the tight white corset that caused her to raise her eyebrows and stare at her lady-in-waiting. "You cannot be serious, Emily. That looks far too small for me. It looks more like an instrument of torture."

"It is designed to accentuate your figure, my lady." The elderly servant stated.

"It looks more like that is going to crush my liver," Clarissa replied contemptuously.

"Well, if I may say so, my lady," Emily said in a chastising tone. "If you didn't indulge yourself in pastries so much, it wouldn't be necessary."

"Are you telling me that I'm fat, Emily?" Clarissa smirked.

"Normally, you have quite a fine figure, but your father thinks it could be accentuated more. His precise words were that if the prince doesn't feel the desire to take you to the bedroom, he may try to alter the arrangements."

"Marran's beard! I'm becoming the prince's wife, not his whore, Emily!" Clarissa raised her voice before gasping as the two maids pulled the corset tight, causing the Second Lady of Jilrir to grunt in an undignified manner

"My lady, don't blaspheme!" The old maid stated indignantly. "Such language is unbecoming of you."

"My father discussing my activities in my future husband's bedroom with staff is what is unbecoming, Emily," Clarissa said with clear irritation and a desperate desire to breathe.

Further discussion on the matter could not be had for that moment; her bedroom door opened, and her father walked in.

"Can I not even have the privacy to dress without interruption?" Clarissa said, despite being fully covered, albeit in what was considered undergarments.

The baron's thick eyebrows narrowed. "We're not going to start this day with your attitude, Clarissa Maine! You take far too much liberty with that mouth of yours."

"Oh, now it's inappropriate for me to speak to my father?" she replied snippily.

He stepped up to her, his no-nonsense expression in full force. "Today, I am not your father, Lady Clarissa. Today, I am your Lord and Master, the Baron Maine of Jilrir, and in the presence of His Royal Highness, you will treat me as such."

Clarrisa dropped into an exaggerated curtsey, causing one of the maids to lose grip of the cord that tightened the corset, causing it to slip open again. "As you wish, master."

Azrael Maine sighed with frustration. "Clarissa, I am stressed enough about this visit without you adding to it with your sarcastic whims. You will greet and treat the Crown Prince with the utmost respect, and you will curb your tendencies to make flippant and unbecoming comments."

"Surely my future husband should know what he's getting," Clarissa added syrup to her words to increase the sarcasm.

"Yes, well, let's allow your husband to discover your propensity to speak above your station *after* the wedding."

"Now, who's being sarcastic, Daddy. I clearly learned from the best," she said in a strained voice, as once more the maids pulled the corset in with Emily gripping her shoulders so she wouldn't move whilst they tied it off.

Maine took a step forward. "I am warning you, Clarissa. If you mess this up today, I will make your life a living hell."

"You mean more than it is?" Clarissa snorted.

The two maids and Emily suddenly jumped back in fright as Azrael moved forward rapidly, gripping his daughter by the back of the neck and pulling her face towards his. "You underestimate me, Clarissa. This is the most important deal in my life, and it's going to send the House of Maine to the top of the league. Fuck this up for me, and as Marran is my witness, I will make you *suffer*."

Genuine fear filled the heart of Clarissa Maine as he stared back in disbelief at her father's aggressive stance. "Understood, my Lord," she responded quite meekly.

He released his hand, shoving her back slightly. "Messengers have arrived to inform us that Prince Campion and his retinue are but hours away. I will be meeting him at the west gate. Ensure you are looking your best in the forecourt before we return and be on your *best* behaviour."

He turned on his well-tailored heel and strode from the room, slamming the door behind him. In silence, Emily and the maids helped her into her gown.

***

The arrival of Prince Campion was a major event for the city. The palace and the city guard joined forces to clear the West Road of citizens, forcing them to close their shops and businesses. Officers donned their dress uniforms, and members of the household retainers joined Baron Maine as he rode his horse down to the south gate to greet the royal carriage.

"Well, you certainly scrub up well, sister." Lord Clarence grinned at her as she stepped out of the front door and joined him on the forecourt. He was dressed in full military regalia, in the colours of the house, red and black. It was purely ceremonial, as his position as captain of the Ithian army was largely ceremonial in nature. The only son and heir of Azrael Maine would not be permitted to risk his life and go anywhere near combat, not that there had been any military engagements in many a year.

Clarissa shot him a glare, but there was no animosity in the look, for she could never be angry at her brother, whose heart was so kind and loving she couldn't imagine how he could rule Ithia. "You're looking pretty dapper yourself, Flubber," she responded, using the pet name that she'd had for him since she was a child. Her smile diminished as she looked at the gate in the surrounding wall where her doom was about to arrive. She felt her brother's arms slip around her shoulder and pull her against him.

"How are you feeling, sis?"

She let out a weary sigh. "Like the hangman is about to come and get me for my execution, if I must be honest," she muttered.

"Oh, it's not going to be that bad, I promise you," he said, trying to sound reassuring but failing miserably.

Clarissa sneered. "I was like seven the last time I saw the prince. I hope he's turned out pleasing to the eye. He was quite scrawny and feeble if I recall accurately."

Clarence smirked. "Your penchant for the rough and big types is rather unfortunate since men of our standing are hardly used to manual labour, my dear sister."

"Indeed." Clarissa gave a wistful sigh as she thought back to the men of the city she had come to know on her unpermitted excursions outside of the great house. "It's all over, Flubber."

"What is?" he frowned.

Realizing he had no concept of what she was talking about, she flushed slightly and quickly deflected. "Oh, my life here with the family."

"I'm going to miss you, baby sister."

It caused a grin to cross her face. She looked up at him, kissed him on the cheek, and said, "I'm going to miss you too, Flubber." She squeezed his hand and forced herself to sound positive. "You must come to Aranar and visit me regularly."

"It's not going to be the same without you here," Clarence sighed.

Clarissa smirked. "Are you going to cry, you big baby?" She teased as he saw his eyes moisten slightly. Yes, Clarence was far too soft to be a Baron, and she feared for him when he did finally succeed to her father's seat, but right now she had her own problems, and it was not like he would have any say in her brother's future.

"Don't be daft, Clarissa," Clement said defensively, but wiped the corner of his eye.

"Let her go, Clarence." A sharp voice came from behind them. "It is hardly appropriate for the Crown Prince to see you clinging to your sister as if you don't want to let her go." He immediately released her at the sound of their stern mother, who came out of the front door of the house. She was possibly more intimidating than her father. She was dressed in a formal blue dress with a high collar that covered her neck and shoulders. Clarissa had never seen her mother looking anything but immaculate, and this was no exception. Lydia Maine stepped in between them, assuming her position, ready to meet the Crown Prince. She glanced briefly at her daughter, then back at the gate. "I expect you to be on your best behaviour, Clarissa. Do not embarrass me today." The ice in her tone was chilling.

"Yes, yes, daddy has already given me the lecture." Clarissa rolled her blue eyes.

"We mean it, Clarissa."

"I promise you, Mummy, that I will be as nice and sweet as a Vargan feffer." She replied with fake cheerfulness, referring to the Goddess of Virtue.

"Oh, I don't think we need to go that far, Clarissa." Her mother snorted. "No man wants to marry a servant of the Goddess of Virtue." She turned to face her daughter and undid the top three buttons of the dress, revealing her cleavage, which had been accentuated by the corset pushing her breasts up.

"Mother, is it your wish that I meet my future husband looking like an upper-class strumpet?" Clarissa said with mock indignation.

"Don't be so crude, Clarissa." Lydia curled her lip. "There is nothing wrong with accentuating one's qualities. When it comes to matters of love, men think with their manhood, not their brains, and first impressions count."

"Maybe I should undress completely and let him know what will be available to him?" Clarissa raised an eyebrow.

Lydia Maine sighed. “Clarissa, you are not as amusing as you think you are. No one wants an amusing wife.”

“And I don’t want a husband who doesn’t find me amusing. Now that’s a problem.”

“Only if you believe this is about you, child.” Her mother sighed. “It is not. This is about the House of Maine, your family, and you will behave, am I understood?”

Clarissa sighed. “Yes, Mummy!”

“How many times do I have to tell you. Don’t call me Mummy.” Lydia sneered. “It’s so common and vulgar.”

“Sorry, my lady,” Clarissa smirked and curtsied.

“You are impossible, child.”

Clarissa turned back to the gate as she watched the palace guard start to line up from the gate towards the house as an honor guard, indicating that the prince’s arrival was imminent. Clarence gave her up one last long, lingering, hopefully reassuring smile, and the shout went up. “Open the gates!”

The gatekeeper and his assistant went to each side of the gate and rolled it back on its wheels, and the sound of the clip-clopping of hooves and the trundling of a carriage could be heard. Her father rode in sitting upright with his back straight, looking all the part as the Baron of Ithia. His own guard followed behind, and then the guard of the prince. The courtyard was not large enough for a procession to enter, so her father rode up to the steps closest to where his family was standing. His guards turned off to line up outside the house on either side of them, and then the royal guard stopped in front of the First Family, and the carriage came to a halt. A page ran down with the block that he then placed before the door of the carriage to act as a step for the prince, and then opened the door.

As Clarissa's eyes alighted with interest on the tall, handsome, broad-shouldered man who stepped out dressed in full military regalia, she couldn't help but feel the stirring of attraction. Maybe this wasn't so bad after all. But her heart sank as she realized he was not the prince when he turned and helped down a thin, effeminate looking man who did not match his portraits at all. Prince Campion was not unattractive, but there was something not quite right. He had soft, feminine features, which some may find appealing, but Clarissa did not. She preferred the more rugged look. Men who had seen life. Her thoughts immediately went to Kevin Kurdow and his muscular physique, along with his stubbly beard.

"Welcome to the House of Maine, Your Highness." Her father's voice boomed out across the courtyard as the Crown Prince approached them, escorted by the handsome man.

"Yes, well, that journey was bloody awful." The Crown Prince said as he stepped up and shook the baron's hand.

Her father bowed before releasing it. "I am sorry to hear that. Maybe we can make up for it with the comforts of my home. We have a meal prepared for you, but first, let me introduce you to your bride." He took Clarissa by the elbow and pulled her forward. As expected, she gave a neat, well-trained curtsy, and in return, Prince Campion bowed.

"Absolutely delighted to meet with you, Lady Clarissa," he said, but his tone was far from delighted, and his expression was one of disinterest.

"Likewise, Your Highness, it is such a delight to meet my fiancée at last." Her father shot her a look, wondering whether she was being sarcastic. Yes, living with Clarissa constantly made him suspicious of her intentions behind her words.

However, the Crown Prince didn't appear interested as his eyes alighted on Clarence. "And who is this fine fellow?" He said much more enthusiastically.

"Allow me to introduce my son, the Second Lord of Jilrir, Clarence Maine," the baron advised.

Campion immediately stepped away from Clarissa and, with a wide smile, shook her brother's hand. His eyes lit up, and his smile seemed more genuine than the one he'd given her. Her brother bowed and took the prince's hand, looking equally pleased to see him. Clarissa looked up at her father and instantly saw an uncomfortable look in his eyes at the interaction between their royal guest and her brother. He noticed her looking, and instantly his expression went passive. "Please come inside, your highness. We have a table laid for you," he said.

The prince smiled up at her father. "Most excellent, I'm quite famished." He glanced back at Clarence with a beaming smile. "Will you be joining us?" It seemed to be a rather foolish question, for obviously the Second Lord of Jilrir would join the honoured guest, but as the prince stepped up to the door with Clarence at his side, that uncomfortable look returned to her father's face.

# CHAPTER THREE

## *The Prince's Man*

No expense had been spared for the welcoming feast of Prince Campion. It was held in the grand hall, rather than the typical dining room, to accommodate a large number of guests. Anyone who was anybody had been invited. There were representatives from other provinces, government officials, and, of course, the wealthier merchants who resided within Jilrir. Azrael Maine would sit at the head of the table with his wife on one side and the prince on the other. Next to his wife would sit Clarissa, and next to the prince would be Clarence. So it was that Clarissa Maine was unable to even talk to her new fiancé, finding herself sandwiched between her mother and the handsome young man who had arrived with the prince. As she took her seat, she gave a stifled cry of pain.

"Do you need assistance, Lady Clarissa?" asked the handsome man with some concern.

"No, no, sir. It is simply that the latest Jilrir fashions are not designed to fit a human. They require my organs to be moved into my chest in order to work, making it inflexible to sit down."

He smiled. It was a nice smile. An attractive smile. She found, despite her growing bad mood, that she returned it genuinely as she stared into his large brown eyes. The young man offered his hand to her. Looking down at it, she said, "In order to take that, I would have to turn further towards you. Please don't make me do that. No offence, but my seams may rip. Do you have a name, sir?"

"Richard Kyle." He chuckled.

"And what is it you do, Richard Kyle?"

"I am the Prince's Man."

She raised an eyebrow and glanced down the table at the prince, who was animatedly chatting with Clarence. She looked back at Richard with a raised, questioning eyebrow.

Kyle flushed slightly. "The role means I serve him as bodyguard, houseman, and valet," he paused. "And only in that capacity," he said intently, getting a little flustered.

Clarissa smirked and gave him a single nod. "Understood, Sir."

"Oh, please call me Richard, all my friends do."

"Oh, we are to be friends? Well, that's nice." Clarissa smirked slightly. "In that case, Richard, please call me Clarissa." Clarissa glanced back down at her fiancé again and gave a long, weary sigh. "Is he even *remotely* interested in women?"

"I'm not sure what you mean, my lady." Richard shifted uncomfortably in his seat, and to avoid her gaze, he looked out at the servants who were bringing in the first course.

"Very well, let me rephrase the question." Clarissa persisted. "Upon my marriage, will my husband's visits to my bed chamber go beyond the requirement to consummate and conceive?"

Richard tensed, hesitated, then let out a long sigh. "That, my lady, will be most unlikely."

Clarissa sighed too. "Understood, Richard."

At this point, her mother leaned towards her, not having heard the quiet conversation between her and the prince's man. "You may as well do those buttons back up, my dear. The prince seems more enamored by your brother."

Clarissa once more glanced down the table, and her eyes widened as she realized her brother appeared just as enamored by the prince. She turned a little pale and felt a little sick, fearing for her sibling. For a man to lie with another man was a capitol offence in the land. Not that such laws affected people of her social class. If her brother were to take a male lover, a blind eye would be turned to it, with the utmost consideration being to ensure it does not become public knowledge.

"Well, they do say my brother looks like me," Clarissa responded, but her mother clearly did not appreciate the joke. A hopeful thought then suddenly occurred to her. "Does this mean the wedding is off?"

"Oh, don't be foolish, child. He does not have to be attracted to you to be married to you."

The seeds of doubt that stirred within her now started to grow into something more.

The rest of the feast was your typical quality fare with several courses of delicacies from throughout the land, especially those that would be rare to find in the Province of Ithia and the City of Jilrir.

For the entertainment, dancers came on, along with jugglers, magicians, and the like. Clarissa paid them little heed, deep in thought about the clearly miserable life she was about to go into. The prince himself also paid little heed, continuing to chat away with her brother.

As the evening progressed, a small quartet of musicians struck up a tune. She saw her father lean over to the prince and whisper something in his ear. The prince then frowned, leaned forward, and looked down the line at Clarissa before rising from his chair and walking around to the front of the table. "My lady, would you do me the honor of joining me in the opening dance?" He said with little interest.

Clarissa smiled, dabbed her mouth with her napkin, and Richard rose to withdraw her seat for her as she stood up. She walked around to the front of the table, where the prince bowed low, and she gave the perfect curtsy. He took her hand and led her to the center of the room as the quartet struck up some music that was slow but not intimate. The elite of Jilrir looked on, and with their right arms raised and palms touching, the couple began a dance, moving around each other and occasionally turning to switch hands as they slowly circled in gentle movements. As appropriate, Clarissa kept her eyes upon him, although whenever they turned in a manner that he was facing the head table, his eyes would flicker towards her brother.

They did not speak even though this was supposed to be an opportunity for them to get to know each other. He was clearly not interested, and she had no idea what to say. The halfway mark of the dance was the point where others were permitted to get up and join them. As the music finished, no one really noticed that the noble couple simply bowed or curtsied and made their way back to their seats.

"Your Highness!" Richard Kyle called out, and the prince turned back to him with a questioning look. "The gift, sire!"

"Ah, yes," the prince reached into his pocket and pulled out a necklace of flawless diamonds. He looked up at Clarissa. "Turn around if you please."

Clarissa complied and lifted her hair so he could place the necklace on her. "A gift of my love." The prince said in a bored monotone voice, reciting something he had memorized. "Like our union may it never be broken." And as it clipped into place, he sauntered off back to his chair and Clarence.

Clarissa stared after him in disbelief as she returned to her own seat. "I can't do it." Clarissa thought once more, imagining a miserable life closeted in Aranar with ladies in waiting only being rolled out for formal occasions, whilst her husband lavished his attentions on some male lover. To be shut in and never tread the streets of the city among the people...

"My lady?" she heard Richard say, concerned, realizing she had spoken her thoughts aloud.

"Oh, sorry. Excuse me, Richard, I need to go powder my nose," she said, almost sounding flustered.

"Just where do you think you're going?" Her mother said haughtily as she rose from her seat. Richard rose too as etiquette demanded.

"When nature calls, mother, one must answer," she replied curtly.

"Be quick about it, young lady." Her father, overhearing them, stated.

"If one had not forced me into this device of torture and oppression." She indicated her dress. "One could make haste, father, but alas, I will be awhile."

Emily, seeing her mistress heading out of the room, hurried after her. Once in the corridor, Clarissa broke into a run. It wasn't as if she had any sort of plan. Indeed not. All she knew was that she had to get out of there and get out of this damn marriage. She started to undo the rest of the buttons of her dress as she raced up the stairwell to her room. She was already pulling it down from her shoulders as she raced through the door. She let it fall to the ground and stepped ungracefully out of it, fumbling at the ties of that damn corset. She opened a drawer on her vanity and pulled out the soldier's knife that she had carried when she left the premises, just in case. She made short work of cutting ties and felt that tingle of relief as the restriction left her body, just as Emily came in the door.

"Lady Clarissa! What do you think you're doing?" The old woman said in shock.

"Go away, Emily, you did not see this," Clarissa said aggressively as she slid the little drawer on wheels that she kept under her bed and pulled out the working-class street clothes that she wore on her little adventures.

"Your father would skin me alive... literally ... if I permit you to do this."

"I am not marrying that man, Emily."

"Where are you going to go?" Emily's voice grew in volume.

Clarissa snorted as she pulled on the pants. "If I were to tell you that my father would know before I reached the gate."

"I can't let you do this, my lady." The handmaiden was quite shrill now. "I will go get your father if you do not come back to the hall."

"Don't task me, Emily." Clarissa snapped, but the old lady was already headed for the door. She was surprised by her own action when she stepped up behind the old woman and, bringing up the soldier's knife, she wrapped her arm around the old lady and held the blade to her throat. "Come with me," she said, not exactly giving the old lady a choice as she dragged the terrified woman over to her closet. Still gripping her, she opened it with her left hand and pushed the old lady inside, closing the door behind her. She grabbed up a hairbrush from the vanity and slipped it into the handles as a lock.

The old lady started immediately banging, but this only hastened Clarissa's speed as she pulled on her shirt over her head and tucked it into her pants. She then sat on the side of the bed, hastily pulling on her boots, tying them, and finally placing the wide-brimmed hat on her head as she headed for the window. Emily started to scream as the second lady of Jilrir climbed out onto the trellis and headed down swiftly, jumping the last few feet to hasten her departure. She didn't know where she was going. She didn't even have any provisions for the road, nor did she even think that she might leave Jilrir. Getting off the grounds of the Great House was all she thought of. She scanned around the garden for any signs of life, and confident the coast was clear, she hurried around to the garden at the back of the house. She ran across the grass towards the back gate, but suddenly froze as a deep voice called out to her.

"Halt, who goes there?" She turned, surprised to see Richard Kyle standing on the porch with a pipe in his hand. She had no idea that the misfortune of his having stepped out for a smoke would, in fact, turn out to be a most fortunate turn of events.

She did not respond and broke into a run, but he swiftly chased her, shouting, "Stay where you are, boy." A hand gripped her collar and spun her around to face him. Startled, he suddenly let go as he found himself looking at the pale yet fair face of Clarissa Maine.

"My lady, what is this?" He asked in utter confusion.

"I'm not marrying that fop," she shouted as her hand went to the back of a belt where she had the knife kept. She didn't know what she was thinking. Was she going to kill him to get away? Surely not.

"Trust me, I understand, but you know what this will entail?" Richard said, his voice firm yet clearly understanding her distress.

"That he will marry my brother?" Clarissa replied sarcastically.

"This will be taken as a grievous insult," Richard said determinedly. "It will cause a rift between the palace and the House of Maine. Do you truly want that?"

"No, I do not, but when has my father ever concerned himself about what I want or what is best for me. I'm just a pawn in the game of politics, and he has no consideration for my welfare, so why should I have a concern for his?"

He gripped her arm. "You are coming back with me before you make a foolish mistake that you will regret."

She struggled to break free before stopping suddenly and staring up into his eyes. "Unhand me before I start screaming rape."

Startled, he instinctively let go, and once more Clarissa broke into a run and out through the back gate. The only sound aside from her heavy breathing and footfalls on the cobblestones was the Prince's Man calling after her. Yet he did not pursue.

Clarissa did not take the back alleys as she normally would. She favored speed over discretion. Between Emily and Richard, the household would know swiftly that she had run away. Another fear started to come over her as she realized she had acted emotionally and without forethought. She could have planned her departure; it was not like the wedding was today. It had merely been a state visit and more of a publicity event. She should have taken her time and planned out this flight, but would she have actually done it? It was a question that she would never be able to answer. She even considered turning back, but the news of her flight had probably already reached her father, and he would most certainly ensure that she never had the opportunity to do it again.

It was almost on instinct that she ran down South Street toward the Fatted Calf, the place she most frequented during her midnight sojourns into the city's underworld. She made a quick decision to visit Kevin Kurdow. She was unsure how he could possibly help, and she was equally concerned that enlisting his help might put him in danger, but what else could she do?

As she reached the door, she stopped for a moment to rest her hands upon her knees and catch her breath. She did not want anyone to see that anything was awry as she entered. She looked back down the street to see if anyone was pursuing her, but there was no one, at least not anyone she could see. She recalled the previous night when the royal guard had turned up here and knew full well that she couldn't stay long, as this was potentially now the first place they would come, thanks to Emily.

So it was as she stepped into the smoke-filled bar of the Fatted Calf. Clarissa Maine greeted the regulars, whom she recognized with her normal smile, as she passed them. She saw Kevin behind the bar serving ale, and as his head rose to see her, his eyes lit up, and a smile crossed those chiseled features.

She rested her elbows on the bar and placed her chin upon her fists as she looked up at him. "Whiskey," she said with a weak smile, but he was already getting it. She downed it in one and slipped the glass back to him, where he was already waiting to pour her second. "I'm in a spot of bother, Kevin." He raised his eyes from the shot glass and looked at her questioningly. "The city authorities are after me, and this time I don't know what to do."

He didn't miss a beat. "Let's go out back and talk." He waved to one of the barmaids to take over, then headed towards the door. Clarissa quickly went around the bar and followed him out. Maddie, who was on the upstairs balcony, just coming out of a room with a punter, saw them. With her natural interest in sticking her nose into other people's business, she quickly kissed her client on the cheek, waved goodbye, and hurried down to follow them.

"I am on the run, and I don't know what to do," Clarissa told Kevin.

He had genuine concern in his eyes. The attraction between the pair was no secret, and he cared for her. "I'd hide you here, but my mother's not gonna wear it." Ethel Kurdow, Kevin's mother, had owned the bar tenancy ever since his father passed away a few years earlier and was quite the shrew.

"I appreciate that, and I wouldn't involve you in my trouble at all if I had a choice. If you are caught assisting me, you may very well hang in the courtyard of the House of Maine."

"The Maines are involved?" This came from Maddie, who came barreling in through the door, startling them.

"It's a long story, but there is a possibility that they will come here looking for me. I need to get out of here and find somewhere to go. Have any of you got any ideas?"

"You could always go to the Marran temple and ask for the Call of Sanctuary; they will not turn you over," suggested Kevin.

"Oh, come now, Kevin." Maddie harrumphed. "The Marran church does not harbor criminals, just those it believes have been unjustly treated. What is it you did that caused you to become embroiled with the House of Maine?"

Clarissa snorted. "I was born. No. Don't worry about it; there isn't enough time; they could be knocking on the door any minute."

"Your best bet would be to get out of Jilrir and lie low for a bit before you come back." Maddie pondered.

"But where should I go?" Clarissa implored.

"Well, I can tell you right now that if you have upset the House of Maine, you will be listed as a state enemy," Maddie warned. "Wanted posters of you will be up anywhere, like Malint, Regor, or Hayburn."

"How about Heron Bay?" Kevin directed the question to Maddie, who pondered it and nodded.

"Would be a good start at least."

Clarissa also pondered this. She wanted to tell them that she was not the gang lord she had made out to be, but something made her hold back. If she were to reveal now that she was actually Lady Clarissa, the Second Lady of Jilrir, that would raise a multitude of questions and potentially erode the trust and support of her friends, whom she needed more than anyone else right now.

# CHAPTER FOUR

# On the Lam

"Heron Bay is five or six days away from here. Where would I get a carriage?" Clarissa considered.

Her two companions stared at her. A grin crossed Kevin's face. "And since when did you become Lady Muck?"

"What do you mean?" The lady frowned.

"You do what everyone else does, Clarissa." Maddie chuckled. "You walk. Have you never left Jilrir?"

Clarissa shrugged. "Well, I've been to the trading post Nethili and the Library of Ternal, but other than that, no."

"And you went in a carriage?" Maddie said suspiciously, causing Clarissa to flush slightly.

"Look, I don't have time for this." Clarissa deflected. "I need to head out now. Kevin, can you please spare me some supplies?"

"That shouldn't be a problem. You have the purse, I take it?" Kevin smiled. "Mum will have a fit if I just give it to you!"

"Will this cover it?" Clarissa reached down to the purse that hung from her belt and pulled out several sivs.

Kevin bit one of the coins more out of habit than a lack of trust in the young woman. "Wait here, I'll pack you a bag."

"You can't go alone, Clarissa," Maddie said once Kevin had gone into the larder.

"It doesn't look like I have much choice, Maddie."

"I could come with you." The old whore said casually, like they were off on a picnic.

Clarissa raised an eyebrow questioningly. "I would be glad of your company, but *why*?"

Maddie shrugged her shoulders and sighed. "I'm getting older, Clarissa, and with age, spreading your legs does not pay as much. I want to do something interesting before I die of syphilis or something."

"I'll come too," said Kevin, stepping back into the room.

"Don't be silly, Kevin, your mother would kill you," Clarissa said, not taking him seriously.

"That's just the point, isn't it?" He shrugged. "I'm not really going to have a life here until my mother passes and I inherit the tenancy, and considering she's only fourteen years older than me, that's a fuck of a long time."

Clarissa looked at him with concern, but couldn't hide her grin. "I don't know how dangerous this road is going to be. I really can't put you both at risk like this."

Maddie chucked. "You're not putting us at anything. We are simply taking a trip to Heron Bay. You lie low, and eventually, the state will give up looking for you, and you can come back."

Clarissa bit her lip, highly doubting that her father would *ever* give up looking for her, but she couldn't say that. No, she would go with them to Heron Bay and see what she would see.

She watched as Kevin went over to a small closet and pulled it open. He pulled out a sword and a weapons belt. He smirked as Clarissa looked at him in surprise. "It was my father's. He was a soldier before retiring and taking over the Fatted Calf. The South Road to Heron Bay is dangerous, filled with highwaymen and the like."

"That's all well and good, but can you use it?" Clarissa said, her tone almost patronizing.

Kevin scowled at her. "While I'm no master swordsman, my dad taught me a few things in my youth."

"Do you have another?" Clarissa asked.

Kevin smirked. "Do *you* know how to use it?"

Clarissa grinned back at him. "Well, I'm no master swordswoman, but my brother taught me a few things in my youth." She said, parodying him. This was not strictly true, as Clarissa had not received any formal military training, but she had frequently accompanied her brother when he was required to learn the sword, bow, and knife as a future military leader.

"I do not, but I have this," he turned and pulled out a rather basic-looking crossbow and handed it to her. Now this was more like it. Clarissa had practiced with the use of a crossbow and an actual bow, for that matter. Archery was not just for war; it was also a sport.

"I'll take that." Clarissa grinned, and he handed it to her before also handing her a quiver of quarrels. She slipped both over her shoulder. But before anything else could be said, there was a crashing sound from the bar. The three spun around towards the closed door, which they could not see through, and they could not see what was going on, but the voices were audible, though they could not make out the words.

Kevin grabbed Clarissa's arm and pulled her towards the back door with Maddie in close pursuit as they headed outside. They went around the side of the inn and onto South Street, giving them a direct line to the southern gate. They did not see the man seated upon the horse outside the inn, but they heard him.

"Halt in the name of the king!"

In the name of the king? This was Jilrir! Guards only called out in the name of the House of Maine. Clarissa spun and looked back, unable to make out the features in the darkness, but she didn't wait. She turned and ran, with Maddie at her side and Kevin taking the rear so that he could turn around in case of a fight.

She could hear the running footsteps behind Kevin, slowly catching up. The man dismounted and began pursuit. She did not see the young innkeeper's son stop and turn, drawing his blade. It was only when she heard the clash of metal that she came to a halt and spun around. Kevin was valiantly trying to fight off the cloaked man. Clearly, he was out of the mystery man's league. Her heart was racing as she pulled the crossbow from her shoulder, slotted in a quarrel, and drew the drawstring back. Could you really shoot someone? She guessed she was about to find out as she raised the weapon.

"Lower your weapon, or as Marran is my witness, I *will* shoot you," she cried out.

The man backed away, as did Kevin. Clarissa moved forward, and she gasped as she found herself looking at Richard Kyle's handsome features.

"My lady, you are certainly a surprise." He called to her. "Your father has called out the entire guard to pursue you."

"And since when did you serve with the palace guard of the House of Maine, Sir?" Clarissa sneered.

"I do not. I'm here at the courtesy of your father and the Crown Prince." He stepped forward, but Kevin stepped between them.

Richard glared at him. "I have no desire to harm you, boy, but I will if you stop me from speaking with the Lady Clarissa and will not lose sleep over it."

"*Lady* Clarissa?" Kevin looked most confused.

At his side, Maddie chuckled. "I knew it! She's a nob."

Clarissa ignored them, her eyes fixed upon Richard Kyle. Her weapon was still levelled at his face. "You bring him harm, sir, and it will be the last thing you ever do."

"How far did you think you're going to get, my lady? Your father has already ordered the north-south, east, and west gates to be closed, ensuring you do not exit. Could you please explain why you are doing this?"

"I told you why. Would you want to be tethered to the Crown Prince?" She sneered. Kevin exclaimed in confusion, and Maddie continued to chuckle.

There was a long pause before Richard Kyle replied in a dejected voice. "I *am* tethered to the Crown Prince."

"Crown Prince?" Kevin's voice rose as more of what was being said began to unnerve him.

"You do not sound pleased about it, Richard." Clarissa challenged.

"Like you, I have to do my duty; it doesn't mean to say I have to like it." Richard scoffed.

"Why do we have to do our duty?" Clarissa said in frustration. "I did not ask to be born the daughter of the House of Maine."

"The daughter of the Baron?" Kevin was almost shrill. "You are Clarissa *Maine*?"

Both Clarissa and Richard ignored this. "And I did not seek to be in the service of the king or the Crown Prince, but my family has been retainers to the monarchy for these three generations. Now I *will* do my duty." Richard shouted.

"That is your choice, but I am not going back," Clarissa responded.

"And that is *not* your choice, Clarissa. I am duty-bound to take you back. If I were to let you go and the Crown Prince found out, it would be me who would be hanged for disobeying orders."

"Well, Sir, we appear to be at an impasse because I'm not going back and I'm not lowering this weapon until you concede defeat." Clarissa gripped her weapon even tighter.

"You don't have to tell the Crown Prince you saw her, you idiot," put in Maddie.

"You wish me to dishonor myself with a lie, madam?" Richard scowled.

"You dishonor yourself by being the lackey of the Crown Prince." Clarissa snapped. "You're chasing a girl who simply doesn't want to get married. Aren't you a big, brave boy?"

"Well, you're too late to do anything, Clarissa," Kevin said softly, indicating that the two officers who had gone into the Fatted Calf were now approaching. They were her father's men, looking none too pleased.

"Okay, my lady, put the weapon down," the first one said, coming up to stand beside Richard. "You too, boy." He addressed Kevin, who still gripped his sword tightly.

They were trapped; there was no way out unless... To say it was easy for Clarissa to fire that weapon would be a lie, yet she moved the weapon from Richard to the guard and fired. It struck him deep in the chest, and he staggered back, falling to his knees. The other guard was startled and fumbled for his sword, but without taking time to think,

Kevin thrust his weapon into his belly. “Oh fuck, oh fuck, oh fuck! What have I just done?” He cried out.

“You just got yourself hanged, boy,” Richard said with incredible aggravation. Clarissa’s target was already dead, but the man on the floor, stabbed by Kevin, was screaming in agony. Richard looked down at him, then at Clarissa, who was reloading. He sighed and ran the agonized man through the heart with his sword to silence him. Clarissa stared at him wide-eyed, and he stared back. “The entire palace guard is out looking for you. They will have heard this man’s cries and are on their way. Come on, let’s get you out of here.”

Without concern about Kevin, he strode past him and then past Clarissa and Maddie, who looked at each other and then followed him. Clarissa stopped and looked back to find Kevin staring at the dead body in front of him. “Come on, Kevin, we have to go.” He didn’t respond, so she trotted up next to him and grabbed his sleeve and pulled at him until he suddenly came back from his thoughts and ran alongside her.

As predicted, the city gate was closed. Richard reached up and pulled Clarissa’s hat further down over her face. A gate guard stepped in front of him as he approached, accompanied by his small retinue, but Richard simply pulled out a golden medallion bearing the king’s seal, and the guard stepped aside. Whatever orders he had from the baron, a king’s man outweighed that. A small door cut into the gate was then opened, and, as if they were out for an evening stroll across the plains, the party of four went through.

Nothing was said as they walked for about twenty minutes before something occurred to Clarissa. “Richard, aren’t you going back?”

Richard sighed and shook his head. “Unfortunately, no, my lady, because of my impulsive action to help you, I will also see a noose around my neck if I am seen again. I guess I’m coming with you.”

He paused, tilted his head slightly, and asked, "Where exactly are we going?"

"Heron Bay," she replied.

The mismatched group continued down the South Road for about ten minutes before anyone spoke. "We should leave the road," Richard said over his shoulder, looking back at Jilrir's dim night lights. "They will be coming after us, and there is no doubt about that."

He started to move off the road and into the brush, but stopped and looked back when he saw no one following him. They just stood there looking at him.

"We need to talk," Kevin said softly, his eyes fixing on Clarissa.

"I think we should listen to Richard," Clarissa said, unable to return his look. "He knows the strategy of the guard, and it would be wise not to ignore his counsel."

"Fuck his counsel." Kevin's voice rose in annoyance, and his glare never left the Second Lady of Jilrir's face.

"We can walk and talk," said Maddie, although her mood was not quite as bad as Kevin's; she still had obvious concerns. As she stepped off into the brush, following Richard, Kevin never moved and kept staring at Clarissa. Eventually, she just sighed, turned away from him, and entered the brush just behind Maddie.

Kevin came up beside her. "Okay, *Lady* Clarissa, let's hear it."

Clarissa let out a long, weary sigh. "Fine! Yes! I am Clarissa Maine, Second Lady of Jilrir. Happy now?"

Kevin inhaled sharply, but Maddie just chuckled and shook her head. "I thought I'd heard correctly," she said. "Well, bless my soul. I had a feeling you were a toff but not quite that high up."

"You're a fucking Maine?" Growled Kevin

"What do you mean by a *fucking* Maine, Kevin?" Clarissa snapped.

"You know what I mean," he muttered.

"No, Kevin, I don't." Clarissa stepped up to him, her fists pressed tightly onto her hips. "Do you have a problem with my family?"

"Well, apparently not as much as you appear to," he sniped.

"He's got a point there," Maddie chuckled.

"Well, there is a big difference between me having issues with my family and other people having issues with them," she snapped, let out a long breath, and said more calmly, "but I take the point. Yes, Kevin, I'm a *fucking* Maine. Born and bred with a silver spoon in my mouth and the title Second Lady of Jilrir. I still want to know if that's a problem?

"Of course, that's a damn problem." Kevin snorted. "The Maines are not going to give up looking for their precious daughter, are they? We're going to be on the run for the rest of our lives, but it's okay for you because if you're caught, you'll just be told 'stop being a naughty girl' while the rest of us are hanged outside the Great House. That's if we survive to get taken back!"

"I didn't ask any of you to come." Clarissa pouted. "You can't blame me for you being in this situation."

"I thought your troubles were the criminal kind," Kevin snorted. "Not the pissing off the fucking son of the king."

"It's not too late for you to go back." Clarissa protested. "The only witnesses to what happened back there are right here, right now."

"Do you want me to go back, *milady*?" Kevin scowled into her face.

"I don't care either way." She lied. She always enjoyed being around Kevin. "And don't call my lady. Call me Clarissa, like you always have."

"Oh no, I know my place." Kevin sighed and forced himself to calm down before looking back up at her again. "What the Marran's beard were you doing coming down to the Calf?"

Clarissa shrugged. "It was fun. Life can be incredibly boring when you're stuck in a house, and everything is done for you. I enjoyed the camaraderie of the regulars and not having people bow and curtsy all the time, treating me like me or not the second lady of Jilrir."

"But you *are* the Second Lady of Jilrir, that's *who* you are," Kevin argued.

"It was who I was born as, but it's not who I want to be, and I certainly don't want to be the wife of Crown Prince Campion."

"Now wait a minute," said Maddie with a considerable amount of confusion. "Are you telling me that you gave up being the future queen in order to be on the run?"

"When you put it like that, it sounds really stupid, but there's more to it." Clarissa blushed. "Life as a member of the nobility is not as easy as you think."

Both Maddie and Kevin laughed at that, and even Richard managed to smirk a little.

"Yes, it must be really hard never having to work, never struggling to put meat on the table, and having one of us put your slippers on for you." Kevin teased.

"It's not like that." She paused. "Oh, well, so yes, I suppose it is ... but it's more than that. Literally every day, I had nothing to do. Sit down and sew or write boring letters to my boring cousins. There was no excitement, no adventure."

"Milady," Richard said. "Adventure is great in storybooks, but in reality, it's a hard world out there, and you're going to miss the comforts of the Great House, but it doesn't matter; there is no going back for any of us."

"I'm quite sure Clarissa could go back; they're not going to hang her." Put in Maddie.

"Do not be so sure of that, Madam. She will not just face the wrath of her father for absconding, but she has also humiliated the Crown Prince. He is without a doubt the most arrogant little shit I've ever had the displeasure of working for." There was a look of satisfaction on Richard's face as he said those words. He had never been able to vocalize his criticism of any member of the royal family before. "In the normal course of things, hanging would be his response even for Clarissa. However, your father may petition the king to avoid your execution, but you will have to suffer for the indignity you have just put down upon his son."

It was at these words that the true realization of what she had just gotten herself into started to dawn upon her. Sure, she had thought of ways of getting out of the wedding, but none of them had involved her leaving the family. And certainly, she did not consider an option that would leave her with no way back.

"I'm sorry I got you all into this," she said softly. She felt a tear coming to her eye, and she cursed herself for it. She had always portrayed herself as a tough, couldn't give a shit badass to two of her companions, and now the frailty of being a Lady of Jilrir was exposed. As she looked down at the ground, she felt an arm go around her shoulders, and Kevin pulled her into his side. "It is what it is, milady. I guess harping about it isn't gonna change a thing. " He kissed her on the side of the head and let her go.

"I promise you this. I will make it up to you somehow. All of you," she said.

"You can make it up to me right now by quickening your pace," demanded Richard. "Come on, the more distance we put between here and the city, the better."

# CHAPTER FIVE

## *Freebooters*

Spring in Ithia was generally mild. However, the one thing spring brought was heavy rain. None of them had dressed for travelling, and when, by early dawn, the rain came down upon them, they were quickly drenched. To make it even worse, the canvas bag in which Kevin had stored their provisions was not waterproof, and all but some dried meat was destroyed.

They sheltered under some trees, which barely kept the rain off them. Clarissa sat with her back to one, her knees pulled up to her chest, hugging them tightly as she watched the raindrops fall from the brim of her hat. Richard and Kevin were arguing, something she realized would be an ongoing issue in the days to come.

"What sort of idiot puts provisions in a porous bag?" Richard was saying.

"It's not like I had a lot of time to think about it, Dick." Kevin sniped back.

"Don't call me Dick!" The former Prince's Man snapped. "The name is Richard!"

"Dick! Dick! Dick!" Kevin retorted.

"Don't be so childish!" Richard sneered.

"By the knees of Illya, will the two of you knock it off!" Clarissa shouted.

Richard turned to her. "Well, my lady, your little adventure is over. We are still four or five days away from Heron Bay, and we have no food or water."

"And exactly what do you expect us to do, Richard?" It was Clarissa's turn to snap irritably.

"Well, I suggest you go back and throw yourself on the mercy of your father, and the Crown Prince, or we are going to die out here." He replied.

"You said yourself that returning was not an option," Clarissa growled.

"I wasn't including death from starvation as one of the possible options."

"Can we not hunt or trap?" Asked Maddie, who was in a worse state, as she was wearing only a short dress.

"Of course, do you know how?" Richard retorted.

"Of course not, but I assumed you did. Don't the king and the prince go hunting?" Maddie muttered.

"Indeed, they do, but I don't join in; I just carry his weapons."

"Well, we're not going back, and that's for sure," Clarissa stated firmly.

Although they had left the South Road, they hadn't moved far from it, using the cover of the brush. They still occasionally looked out to use it as a guide to ensure they were heading in the right direction.

They would duck down and hide if any horses or carriages passed, for it was a busy road that led from Jilrir to all locations in southern Ithia.

As she heard one such distant carriage heading in their direction, a thought occurred to her. She quickly dismissed it as a stupid idea.

"We may be able to get there without the food in five days for ourselves on the mercy of the Illyan temple." Richard suggested, "But there is a chance one of the horsemen that passed us is a messenger and that we would be expected to arrive, and they will be on the lookout for you." The carriage grew ever closer, and that silly thought came back into her head. "So, my lady, what do you say?"

Clarissa bit her lip, pondered for a moment, and then got up, grabbing her crossbow. "I say we go replenish our provisions."

"What are you talking about?" Richard scowled, but as she slipped a quarrel into the weapon, his eyes opened wide. Kevin sighed, shook his head, and Maddie giggled.

"From princess to highwayman in a single day, you suddenly have some gall, milady." Kevin rolled his eyes.

"You cannot be serious, my lady," Richard said, stepping towards her as she pulled back the drawstring.

"Isn't it the case that you will be hanged anyway?" Clarissa tilted her head questioningly at him.

"Yes, but..."

"We have nothing to lose." Clarissa shrugged.

"There are always our lives. Carriages do not travel unarmed and unguarded on the South Road."

"Then I suggest we be careful." Clarissa shrugged again. "I am fairly certain that they will only be armed with swords, and I have this, so as long as I stay out of arm's reach, it should be fine." She rested the crossbow against the tree and pulled out a handkerchief with lacy edges. She pulled down her hat and tied it around her nose and mouth so that only her blue eyes could be seen.

"This is crazy, you're going to get yourself killed," Richard advised.

Kevin shrugged. "You said we're going to die anyway, at least it increases our chances of surviving, but Clarissa, you have to understand you may have to shoot."

Richard threw his hands up into the air in resignation. "Give me the weapon, I'll do it."

"Are you an experienced marksman?" Clarissa asked.

"Never used one before, but it can't be that difficult." Richard shrugged.

"I have been trained back when my brother was doing his military training. I joined him, and I'm quite adept with the weapon," Clarissa replied.

"The Land has gone insane." Richard threw his hands up into the air, but Clarissa was already running down the little slope, gripping the weapon with both hands, and Kevin was close behind her, his hand on the hilt of his sword.

All the arguments had made her almost miss the carriage, but she was delighted to see that it was a merchant vehicle rather than a passenger one, stacked with boxes and crates of merchandise heading toward Jilrir. The second lady stepped out onto the road and raised her weapon, and the driver instantly started to rein in the horse. "Easy there, gentlemen," she called out to them as Kevin joined her. "This will all be over very quickly, and no one needs to get hurt."

Richard chose to use some form of tactics and circled round to the back.

Although the two men looked scared, the passenger suddenly brought up a cylindrical object and pointed it at her. She didn't react beyond being curious, but jumped when there was the sound of a small explosion, something she had never heard before, and smoke rose in front of the man's face. She tried to fathom what was going on as she stared up at him. He had turned the object over and was filling it with some power. Then, after a moment, she noticed her shirt turning red around the shoulder, and then a world of pain hit her. "What the hell just happened?" she gasped.

"Marron's beard!" Kevin shouted, looking at her desperately as the blood continued to spread across her garment. As the man started to point the cylinder at her again, she raised her own weapon once more and fired. She wasn't aiming for anywhere specifically, but it struck him in the throat, and his head slammed against the back of the carriage before he slumped and fell from his seat just as Richard pulled the driver from the other side. Clarissa reached under the tassels that ran down the front of her shirt, noticing a small hole in the fabric. She pulled the shirt off her shoulder, and Kevin quickly examined the small hole in her shoulder. "Magic?"

"There is no such thing," Clarissa muttered.

Richard pulled the driver down from the cart and stepped around in front of the horse, dragging him with him. He pushed him down to the ground at her feet and then stepped around to examine her wound. "This is not magic. She has been shot with the foulest weapon ever created."

"Well, apart from a shit load of pain, it's not very effective. I'm still alive." Clarissa winced.

Richard turned her around and looked at the back of her shoulder. "That's only because it's gone straight through you and didn't hit any vital organs. You're going to live, but we need to cauterize that and ensure you don't get an infection. In the meantime..." He pulled the handkerchief from her face, ripped it in two, and stuffed each part in the exit and the entrance of the wound. Clarissa was no longer listening. She was looking over the body of the man who had shot her, and as Richard finished, she stepped over to him. She picked up the small, cylindrical object, which had a handle and a trigger similar to those of her crossbow. "How the hell does this work?"

"You stick a metal ball in one end, fill it with powder, and it strikes a spark, projecting the metal ball after great velocity towards your opponent," Richard advised her.

"What's it called?" Clarissa frowned quizzically.

"A puffer," Richard said.

"Dumb name," Clarissa replied. She reached down and grabbed the pouch with the fire powder, and then found strips of gummed lead balls hanging from his belt and slipped them into her pocket.

"You don't intend to use that abhorrence?" Richard said with some contempt.

"Why shouldn't I?" Clarissa raised an eyebrow.

Richard scowled. "It is a coward's weapon; it gives an unfair advantage against an opponent."

Clarissa pondered this and simply smirked. "I don't want to give an opponent an advantage." She slipped the weapon into her belt and tied the black powder pouch next to her purse. She gave Richard a 'do not you dare challenge me' look, and he just shrugged it off and shook his head.

"I guess we should go see what we have stolen," Kevin said.

Clarissa looked down at the dead man. The man she had just killed. He may have had a family, and he may have been a father whose children now have no income. Guilt started to creep in, but then she thought more about it. He had chosen the job of caravan guard, and he was aware of the risks. Indeed, this was an occupational hazard.

"Lumber," Richard called back, interrupting her thoughts. "It's clearly bloodwood for carpentry; they must have come from Regor because this tree only grows in the west."

"Thank you for the geography lesson, but what we need is food," sneered Kevin.

"Patience, boy. These two needed to eat, and supplies are all but guaranteed." Richard shot him a look.

They found that the packs were stashed behind the seats by the drivers. Richard tossed a bag to Kevin and put one on his back himself.

"So, what do we do with him?" asked Maddie, indicating the quiet man who knelt on the floor with his head down, trying not to draw any attention to himself.

"Let him go, we have what we need," Kevin said

"We should take the cart," Maddie said. "We will travel further for longer."

"I thought we were avoiding the guards along the roads," said Clarissa.

"Well, they're only gonna be looking for you and possibly me," Richard advised. "Miss Maddie and Kevin can ride the carriage. You and I can hunker down in the back if anyone comes along."

"Well, it beats walking and in that case..." She turned to the man on the ground. "It's your lucky day. Get walking." She pointed in the direction of Jilrir.

He scrambled to his feet with his hands together as if in prayer, as he kept bowing towards her. "Thank you, my Lady Clarissa, thank you, thank you." He turned and did a half-run, half-walk thing as he tried to get as far away from them as possible, but as she turned away from him, she suddenly realised something. She looked back at him. He had not gone too far, and she let out a sigh.

"None of you used my name, did you?" she asked the group, pondering.

They stood there looking at each other, and Clarissa cursed under her breath. "Damn it to hell, he recognized me."

"Are you sure?" Maddie frowned.

"He knew my name!"

"But how? Have you met him before?" Kevin asked, not convinced.

"I'm from The House of Maine. Portraits of my family and me hang in every civic building throughout the province. It's not often, but sometimes I'm recognised."

There was a slight pause as she slipped the crossbow off her shoulder. Everyone looked at each other again, and Kevin reached out to stop her. "Does it matter that he recognizes you. The city guard surely knows you've come this way and are looking for you."

"Yes, but he can now describe exactly who I'm with," she muttered.

"Ah!" Kevin pulled his hand away, then stepped back as Clarissa pulled back the drawstring and inserted the quarrel. She pondered using the new puffer, but she probably needed a little practice with that before using it. She raised the weapon and took careful aim.

"Get closer, you're not going to hit him from this distance," Richard said.

She ignored him and fired. The quarrel struck the man neatly in his back, and he fell forward. "I think that was a pretty neat shot."

"He's still alive, my lady." Richard sighed.

Clarissa went to pull out another quarrel, but Richard stayed her hand. "You only have a finite supply of those, and they are completely unnecessary now."

"Well, what do you expect me to do?" Clarissa asked, although she was certain she knew.

"I see you have a knife there," he said, indicating her blade at her boot.

"You expect me to stab him?" She said, feeling a little queasy at the idea of doing something so up close and personal.

"Well, slitting his throat will be more efficient and quicker," Richard stated.

"I'm not sure that I can do that, Richard," Clarissa said in barely a whisper.

Kevin put his hand out for the knife. "I'll go do it," he said, but Richard pushed it aside.

"No, no, Clarissa chose a life on the lam. She's going to have to learn that things are not always as pretty as they are in the Great House."

Clarissa looked at Kevin, hoping that he would argue the point, but he didn't. She took a deep breath, pushed her shoulders back, and strode down the road to where the man was still thrashing about. She pulled out the knife and stood over him a moment. He was lying face down and couldn't turn over due to the shaft protruding from his spine. However, he stopped moving when he could see Clarissa's boots. "I'm so sorry. I don't have a choice," she muttered feebly.

He tried to reply, but a punctured lung ensured that he only coughed up blood instead. Clarissa took several deep breaths, then, with determination, she bent down, grabbed him by the hair, and pulled his head back. Closing her eyes, she sliced the knife across his throat. There was a weird sound, like a sigh. With her eyes closed, she didn't realise this was the air escaping from his throat. It was quickly silenced as blood gurgled up. She rose, turned away, and slipped the life back into its sheath. Only when she was far away from him did she open her eyes.

"That was very brave," Kevin reassured her.

"It was a stupid waste of life," Clarissa muttered.

"There is only one other thing I should mention," Richard said almost mockingly.

"Oh, and what exactly is that?" Clarissa frowned.

"Next time, clean your knife before you put it away." He nodded down towards the sheath, and as she followed his gaze, she saw the blood running down it and onto her trousers.

"Marran's girdle! I'm going to look a right state when we reach Heron Bay," she said, climbing into the back of the cart, pushing away Kevin's hand as he tried to assist her.

Maddie and Kevin went up front, whilst Richard joined her in the back. It took a bit of maneuvering to get the cart to turn around on the road, but it was not long before they were bouncing along toward Heron Bay.

***

The fishing village of Heron Bay was probably one of the smallest communities within the Province of Ithia, if not The Land itself. It was that traditional sleepy town where time just passed without any pressure on its inhabitants.

It lay in a small valley that wasn't visible from the South Road, for as you approached, the gradient grew upwards. The first sight was a hill upon which a relatively small temple stood at its summit. Illyan temples were usually grand affairs, but this one was not built by the Illyans but by people in a bygone age, under circumstances that were no longer known. It was quite plain and perfectly square, with four towers at each corner, and turrets that were only equivalent to being four stories high. Clarissa did not have any particular religious beliefs. Officially, the House of Maine was Marran following the Goddess of

Nature, and she could not help but notice that was quite a contradiction, since her family lived in an overcrowded city where anything green was an incredible rarity.

As the little cart struggled against the load up the hill, Clarissa was now seated between Kevin and Maddie. "A little small for a fortress, isn't it?" She said, unaware of the town's history.

"That's no fortress, milady, post it. That is the Temple of Illya." Kevin said.

"Is it safe to go past them?" Clarissa asked uneasily.

"Why wouldn't it be?" Maddie frowned.

"Oh, my father always complains about the Illyans and their interference in state matters." Clarissa mused.

"Well, if you promise not to get involved in state matters, then we should be fine." Kevin chuckled. "But just to be sure, you'd better get back in the back."

Unable to stand up and turn around, Clarissa had to roll back into the rear of the cart, where she lay down between one of the stacks of lumber. When Kevin suddenly slowed the horse, she became a little bit concerned about what was going on, considering they were not exactly moving very fast to begin with. She then heard a woman's voice.

"Hail and well met, are you here on business?"

"Just making a delivery," Maddie stated cheerfully.

"Indeed, and who do you have to deliver your wares to?" The woman responded.

They hadn't come up with a cover story beyond that they were delivering their stock to the town, and it didn't occur to them that they might be specifically asked who they were delivering to.

Kevin hesitated, and the hesitation grew. Eventually, whoever it was he was talking to became impatient. "Okay, I think we're going to take a look in the back." The woman demanded.

"By what authority?" Maddie growled.

"By the authority that my sword is bigger than yours, Madam," The woman replied, her tone threatening.

Clarissa had turned onto her side, where she lay in the back of the cart and slipped the crossbow from her shoulder. She then lay back on her back again and, using her feet to help, she pulled the drawstring back, then slipped a quarrel in.

"Are you seriously threatening us?" Kevin blustered. "Aren't you supposed to be a priestess?"

"I am indeed a priestess, but we are also responsible for working with the city on maintaining this town's security. Who are you delivering this to is a simple question, but one you cannot answer."

Clarissa turned over onto her belly and crawled up to her knees. She suddenly jumped up, intent on taking out this woman so they could get away, but found her facing the aged priestess in blood red robes and three armed men standing behind her. They all made for their swords as they saw Clarissa aim at the priestess, who looked unfazed and simply raised an eyebrow at her. Realising it would be foolhardy to kill one and be killed by the other three, she lowered the crossbow.

"Well, this is certainly awkward," Clarissa said with a weak smile.

"Put the weapon down and step out of the cart." The priestess said.

Clarissa complied, and stepping over Richard, she said, "You may as well get up. She's got three troopers standing behind her." He did so, smiling weakly at the surprised-looking priestess as the two jumped down and walked around to the front, where Maddie and Kevin stood.

"Is anyone going to give me an explanation?" The priestess asked softly....

# Chapter Six

# *Heron Bay*

The four visitors looked at each other and then back at her, without saying a word. "Okay," the priestess said, for she was a priestess. "Who's in charge of this little party?"

Again, the four companions looked at each other again until Richard said. "I guess she is," and pointed to Clarissa.

Kevin nodded, and Maddie said, "Yeah!"

The priestess took a step forward. "Do you have a name, young lady?"

"Clarissa," Clarissa said, it not occurring to her to make up a name.

"Nice to meet you, Clarissa. I am sister Elsbeth of the Holy Church of Illya, Goddess of Justice. Now we have those formalities out of the way, why are you driving a cart into Heron Bay with no idea where you're actually going?"

"Oh, I know where we're going all right," Clarissa lied. "I just don't believe you have the right to question me."

Elsbeth stepped up eye-to-eye with her. "Oh, we do. We own the pathway you just came up from the South Road; you are on church property."

Clarissa frowned. "Church property? This path is the only way in and out of Heron Bay without leaving the road."

"I am aware of that. I live here," the sister said, sarcastically. "It doesn't change the fact that you're on church property."

"So, everybody within this village or town or whatever you want to call it is answerable to you whether they come or go?" Clarissa sneered.

"Technically, yes, but we only stop people who are not residents of the town."

"How do you know we're not residents?" Clarissa shrugged.

The priestess chuckled, "It's a very small town, and everybody knows everybody." She looked Clarissa up and down. "And generally, residents do not venture out and return covered in blood."

"Well, I don't have a story for you that will satisfy you," Clarissa shrugged more nonchalantly than she actually felt. "So all I can say is I'm going to refuse to answer your questions."

"Then I'll have my men here detain you until the town militia is called." The priestess said.

"Now I *know* you have no right to do that," Clarissa said with a modicum of incredulity. "Such an act would be considered kidnapping without authority from the state."

"I *have* the authority from the Mayor of Heron Bay." Elspeth narrowed her eyes. "Is that good enough for you?"

"No, I'm afraid it isn't. The mayor of Heron Bay requires the authority of the House of Maine because, in reality, the state owns all this land." Clarissa sparred.

"I cannot argue with that, but there is another matter you should consider." The priestess folded her arms. I have the support of the mayor and the militia, and you don't. If I detain you, who's going to complain apart from you?"

Clarissa, seeing no other way out of this, decided to take a gamble. "Fine! My full name and title is Lady Clarissa Maine, Second Lady of Jilrir."

There was a slight pause. "And I'm the Mayor of Hayburn," the priestess smirked, indicating she didn't believe her.

"She speaks the truth," Richard said, stepping up to Clarissa's side.

"And I'm supposed to trust you more than I trust her?" the priestess tilted her head.

"Trust this." He reached into his pocket, pulled out the small medallion, and held it before her.

She looked momentarily confused as the realization came upon her. She looked up at him. "You are an officer of the king?"

"As this indicates."

Once more, she looked at each in turn with some confusion. "Now this is a riddle indeed." She pondered a moment before her shoulders slumped and she sighed. "You had better come inside and meet the head of our order."

Clarissa nodded and followed her through a large oak door into a small foyer. A small stone alcove led to a spiral stairway heading up to the second floor. Sister Elsbeth led them through a corridor that wound round to once more face the south of the building. A young priestess in white sat behind a desk and stood up as sister Elspeth entered. "Is Sister Annalise available?"

The young girl simply turned around and knocked on the door behind her. They heard a woman call out, "Come."

The unusual group of friends stepped into the chamber.

The circular office of the high priestess was grey and austere. Arched windows surrounded the room from floor to ceiling, and sunlight lit the faded mosaic of a red rose on the floor. A desk lay opposite the open door.

"I'm sorry to disturb you, Sister Annalise, but a situation has arisen that requires your attention," Elsbeth informed her.

Annalise smiled. She was a tall, fair-looking woman, younger than the priestess who introduced them.

"Who is it that we have here?"

"This young lady here styles herself as Lady Clarissa Maine, Second Lady of Jilrir." Informed Elspeth. "Yet claims to be delivering blood-wood lumber."

Annalise looked surprised. "Well, we are honoured to have such a noble visitor, but usually we are informed of the arrival of members of the House of Maine." She looked around the assembled group, her eyes mostly alighting on Maddie and Kevin. "Although when they do arrive, their retinue is a little more salubrious."

"Well, obviously, this is not a normal visit," Clarissa replied a little curtly. She had been raised with a distrust of clerics, and that was not going to be dispelled easily. "And it was not my intention to stop here at the Illyan Temple. We simply want to go in and find a room within Heron Bay and continue with our business here."

"Come, take a seat and relax." Ananalise smiled, indicating some formal-looking chairs. "We may be servants of the Goddess of Justice, but I am not going to judge you." She paused and smiled wider. "At least not yet."

"That is not a very reassuring way to put it." Clarissa took the one chair that was in front of the high priestess' desk. The companions looked about and took the seats that were lined against the walls. "Come, Elsbeth will get us some tea, and you can tell me your story. You cannot argue that we are going to be suspicious when you claim to be Lady Clarissa, yet you walk in here in a common man's riding attire covered in blood, which I assume is not your own."

"Well then, you assume wrongly. The blood upon my shirt is my own, but the blood upon my trousers is not. So you're half right there."

The high priestess rose and stepped around the table. "You are wounded? Show me."

Clarissa hesitated, then pulled the clothing down over her shoulder. It stung as Annalise pulled the pieces of the handkerchief from the hole in her shoulder. The priestess then placed her hand over the wound and muttered a prayer. There was a sprinkle of dust like blue lights, and before her eyes, the hole closed and sealed. As if this were all perfectly normal, Annalise returned to her chair as Maddie muttered something to Kevin.

Annalise frowned and sat back, crossing her arms. "You are clearly choosing to be evasive, and evasion implies guilt of some misdeed."

Clarissa looked at the healed shoulder, trying to hold back her amazement, and then leaned forward toward the High Priestess. "It could also mean that I stood up for my rights in that I did not need to be interrogated by the church. My business is my own."

Annalise's smile didn't waver. "Come now, Lady Clarissa, if indeed you *are* Lady Clarissa. You must understand you arrive here with suspicious circumstances, and we want to know the truth."

"The truth is, I want to go into the village of Heron Bay; however, if it is your wish, we will move on. All I ask is that we get to restock provisions for a much longer journey to Regor."

"So, you are not here in Heron Bay with a particular purpose, for you are certainly not delivering bloodwood lumber?" Annalise persisted.

"Do I have your leave to depart, or not?" Clarissa's voice rose. "My father would not be impressed if he received news that you are detaining me against my will."

"Oh, I know Baron Maine quite well, having met him on many occasions." Annalise chuckled mirthlessly. "I'm fairly certain that if you are his daughter, he is not aware you're even here."

"And why do you say that?" Clarissa asked, her anger marred by unease.

"Because he would not let his daughter travel in a lumber wagon and certainly not without at least three to four palace guards at her side. So, either you are lying to me about who you are, or you're here without his consent or knowledge. I'm going to go with the latter because to pretend to be Lady Clarissa whilst dressed like that and, forgive me, the company you keep would be so utterly ludicrous and therefore must be the truth."

Clarissa sighed, biting her lip, and saw nothing for it but to come clean. "Your holiness, I am indeed Clarissa Maine, and, yes, I am here against my father's will, but I am of age, and there is no law that says that I have to remain with my family. He may try to compel me to, and he may even succeed. However, if you delay me here, you are only assisting his search for me, and that is taking sides, which I know the Illyans do not do easily. How I got here is irrelevant, and the manner in which I got here is also irrelevant. I am looking for a temporary sanctuary in Heron Bay, and all we need is a place to lay our heads, gather supplies, and we will be on our way."

"Well, that wasn't so difficult, was it, my dear?" Annalise rose to her feet again. "You are quite correct, you're leaving Jilrir is a family matter, not a legal one, nor a church one. We will not involve ourselves in this matter. However, you have clearly taken that cart without the owner's consent. It must be returned to them. When you depart, please leave it behind, as we will take care of its restoration. I will permit you to stay here for one night, and that's it. Allowing you into the town and giving you succor is also taking a side. Am I understood?"

"You are fully understood; however, we need to get supplies to continue our journey."

"I will give you an escort to take you into town with your servants..." She stopped looking over at Kevin as he raised a hand. "Yes?"

"We are not her servants." The high priestess did not reply; instead, she looked at him, making him feel quite uncomfortable. "I just wanted that understood."

The priestess returned her attention to Clarissa. "Honestly, my dear, I understand nothing about these events or what you're up to. I know enough to know you are not a danger to my church or the town of Heron Bay. That said, I stick to my word; I do wish you to leave on the morrow. We do not wish to face the wrath of Baron Azrael Maine when he finds out we're harboring you in the city. As I said, you can go into the town with an escort. We will then give you quarters for the night and a good breakfast in the morning, and then you will be on your way. Is that acceptable?"

Clarissa rose to her feet, indicating her desire to conclude the conversation. "Acceptable or not, you are not giving me any choice in the matter, so I graciously accept your hospitality for one night and look forward to meeting your escort who will take me into the village." She smiled a sweet, fake smile and gave a slight curtsey before turning and heading back towards the door.

"Damn Illyans," she muttered, but it was only ever heard by Richard as he followed close behind.

***

Heron Bay served two purposes; first and foremost, it was the primary fishing port, supplying Ithia and beyond with a vast array of fish and crustaceans. Its other purpose, one for which it was not intended, was a place of retirement. The little village, with pretensions of being a town, was peaceful and picturesque. There was little to no industry, and the pace of life was slow.

Clarissa Maine had never seen anything like it out of the filthy capitol city in which she was raised. As she stood at the entrance of the Ilyan Temple and looked down the hill, she saw the little cottages and townhouses scattered haphazardly across the green landscape, topped off by the ocean. All she could hear were the gulls flying over, hoping to get a chance at the morning catch. A small, barely maintained pathway led down the hill. It was barely wide enough for two wagons to pass each other. On either side, long grass grew up to about four to five feet, forming a green wall.

"It's so beautiful," Clarissa murmured as she stared down at the picturesque site.

"We certainly enjoy it." Clarissa turned to see a red-robed priestess approaching her. "Hello, I'm Sister Taylor. The high priestess asked me to be your escort into the village."

"You know we're not going to start trouble," Clarissa said, quite offended by the fact that they were going to be escorted.

"Oh, I'm sure you're not. It is just a precaution." She smiled sweetly.

"It's a bloody insult," muttered Kevin.

"Maybe it is, maybe it isn't," Taylor said chirpily. "But it's not my insult, I am merely following the instructions of my superior. If my superior has offended you, take it up with her, but please don't take it out on me."

"Fair enough, Taylor." Clarissa conceded. "I will take you at face value and judge you on your words and actions as we go along."

Despite this being a dig, Taylor simply laughed, "Fair enough, Lady Clarissa, shall we go?"

Clarissa walked ahead with the priestess, but Richard and Kevin were not far behind. Maddie, on the other hand, trailed along, enjoying the sunshine. She had heard the sun always shone in Heron Bay, but she knew that that couldn't possibly be true, yet it belied the onset of summer. As they approached, they could hear the fisherman singing some sea shanty down by the docks being carried back to them on the breeze.

"We need warmer clothing and enough provisions to get us to Regor." Clarissa was telling the priestess.

"Not a problem," Taylor informed her. "We can visit the market and then Samuel's Tailoring and Bootery."

"How is your purse holding out?" Richard asked uneasily. "Even you do not have an inexhaustible supply of coin."

"I have sufficient money for the provisions and clothing, but to be honest, I'm only guessing," Clarissa replied. "It's not like I go out and do grocery shopping for myself." Clarissa untied the purse from her belt and tossed it to him. "See for yourself."

Richard opened it and looked inside; his eyes narrowed with a frown. "This isn't much. We need to give some serious consideration to how we are going to pay our way."

"Let's just get through today, shall we?" Clarissa replied.

The Market Square at the center of the village was insignificant compared to the one in Jilrir. The choices of goods were far fewer, and there was an overabundance of fish for sale.

Calling Samuel's a tailor was quite the misnomer, for clearly his clothing supplies were imported from Jilrir and beyond. Considering the distance, the price matched the convenience or lack of it. Clarissa paid for new coats, and she saw that, indeed, Richard was right, as all she had left was loose change in her purse.

"So, where is it that you intend to go?" The young priestess asked as they started heading back towards the temple.

"As we have already said, we are heading towards Regor," Clarissa told her.

"Yes, indeed, but that is not your ultimate destination, is it?"

Clarissa sighed. "Honest truth, we don't know where we are ultimately going. Wherever the road takes us, I guess."

The priestess' eyes lit up. "That sounds so exciting."

Clarissa's eyebrow raised slightly. "Not happy in your current situation?"

"I am perfectly happy being a priestess, and one does not get called by the goddess unless they are, but it *can* be so boring." Taylor sighed.

"Then why don't you leave?" Clarissa suggested.

"Oh, my dear, one does not leave the service of Ilya." Taylor chuckled. "Oaths are made, and I did this for life and beyond."

"Yes, but there's a big world out there; you don't have to be stuck in this little village," Kevin stated. "There are positively hundreds of Illyan temples throughout the land in much more interesting places than this."

"Oh, you don't like our little village?" the priestess smirked.

Clarissa chuckled, "It's positively beautiful, and maybe when I'm elderly, I might want to retire by the beach, but the tranquilly of this place will soon wear off on me."

Suddenly, Richard gripped her shoulder and pulled her back slightly. She spun around to look at him, but he was staring up the hill towards the temple. "We've got trouble." He muttered.

Clarissa followed his gaze and had a sudden sharp intake of breath, for atop the hill by the entrance sat three horsemen. Not particularly outstanding in these parts, except for the fact that they bore the livery of the palace guard of the House of Maine.

"What's the problem?" asked the priestess with concern.

Clarissa didn't answer her. "Okay, everyone, let's turn around and walk away slowly and not draw attention to ourselves." Her companions complied, but the priestess frowned.

"I'm supposed to take you back," she said with concern.

"Not while those men are there," Richard growled.

"If you don't come back with me, I'll have to go and report it," Taylor said desperately.

"Yeah, that's not happening," said Clarissa almost apologetically as Kevin and Richard stepped up on either side of the priestess and turned her around to face the town once more.

"Keep walking, your holiness," Kevin said with a little hint of intimidation.

The priestess complied, and the group once more ventured back into the town.

# Chapter Seven

## *Lady Luck*

They came across a quaint little tavern, which, unbeknownst to them, was the only tavern in town. As they entered, all the patrons fell silent and stared at them, but it was not at Clarissa and her companions. Ilyan priestesses didn't go into alehouses, and the red-robed priestess stood out like a beacon.

"Grab a table, I'll go get us some drinks," Kevin said as he moved off through the bar, ignoring the stares. As they made themselves comfortable, the conversation started up again around the bar, and interest in them quickly waned.

Kevin returned with a tray of five ales, but the priestess just stared at it when he placed hers in front of her, and she slowly pushed it to the middle of the table.

"Sorry, milady," Kevin said to Clarissa. "I didn't have any coin, and I had to open a tab for you."

"Not a problem, Kevin, and please stop calling me 'my lady.' You've always called me Clarissa, and there is no reason for that to change."

Kevin smirked. "Call it payback for all the bullshit you've given me, milady."

Clarissa simply rolled her eyes and blew the froth from the top of her beer before taking a sip. "How long do you think the palace guard will stay in the town?" She asked Richard.

"That all depends on what the Illyans tell them. If they admit we are here, they will begin searching when we do not return," he advised.

"Then we need to get out of the village as soon as possible," said Maddie.

"That is the only road in and out of the village," Clarissa responded.

"Then we hide, we wait until they've left," Kevin suggested.

"They won't leave if the Illyans tell them that we are in the village," Richard said grimly.

"What do you say, Taylor? Will your people sell us out?" Clarissa asked.

"Well, I wouldn't call it selling you out, but they don't have any particular reason not to tell them," the priestess said defensively.

As the conversation about what to do went on, Clarissa found herself staring out of the window and across to the docks. It was mostly fishing vessels, but the occasional merchant vessel was dotted here or there. Most, however, were vessels out at sea, getting the catch of the day. Another silly idea entered her head, which she quickly dismissed.

"It is not like we know anyone in this village who would help hide us," Richard was saying. "And I'm fairly certain that the baron's men will be very extreme in such efforts."

"Maybe if we split up, it would be less conspicuous," Kevin said. "We could arrange to meet up again when they've left."

"It will be days, possibly weeks, before they give up." Richard dismissed his idea. "This is no highwayman they are searching for. This is Clarissa Maine, the Second Lady of Jilrir."

"Yeah, let's keep our voice down, Dick. We don't want everybody to know." Another round of macho posturing between Richard and Kevin began, and once more, Clarissa found herself looking outside the window, and that silly idea once more ventured into her head.

"Can anyone sail a boat?" At those words, everyone went quiet and looked at her. She turned away from the window and looked at each in turn, a head tilted slightly as she looked at them questioningly. The fact that no one answered gave her her answer. "This is a port. Roads are not the only way out of here."

"We cannot afford passage on a boat," Maddie stated.

"Which is why I asked if any of you knew how to *sail* a boat," Clarissa replied.

"We are less than five days from Jilrir." Richard scoffed. "You are already guilty of murder, and now you wish to add piracy to those crimes?"

"Murder?" The priestess' eyes widened as she stared at Clarissa.

"Oh, he's just exaggerating, dear." Clarissa smiled at the priestess innocently. "Don't worry about it." But she said it a little too hastily to be believable.

"We should hide up and wait till night," suggested Kevin, who was clearly going to be the least objectionable about the idea. "No one's going to be around."

"Considering none of us can actually sail," Clarisa said. "We're going to need some of the crew to stay aboard."

"Oh, so now she wants to add kidnapping." Richard raised his hands in despair and let his head fall back with a sigh of disbelief.

"If you're not going to be helpful, Richard, can you just shut up?" Clarissa said, getting exceedingly frustrated with him.

"I am just trying to point out the foolishness of your idea."

"Come now, Richard. Since you do not have an alternative, the lack of a plan is more foolish, don't you think?" Clarissa chided.

"Yeah," said Kevin, who would have agreed with anything Clarissa said, especially if it was against the pompous royal officer.

"Come on, let's go get a boat." And with that, Clarissa jumped out of her seat.

"We don't even have a plan," Richard said, startled. "Why are you always so impulsive?"

"What's to plan. We find a boat. We take the boat and sail down to Hayburn. Keep it nice, keep it simple." Clarissa tossed some coins down on the table for the beers.

"They will not give up that boat that easily, milady." Richard followed her out into the street.

"We shall see what we shall see."

The small group headed down to the dock. They had almost forgotten about Taylor, the priestess who just followed along, not knowing what else to do.

There were multiple boats long the jetty of various shapes and sizes. However, there were no big galleons or even the bigger trawlers. Heron Bay just wasn't built for them.

The mismatched group drew attention solely because they were armed. Richard and Kevin with their swords, and Clarissa with her crossbow and puffer. It was not as if no one was ever armed when they went down to the docks of Heron Bay, but it was extremely rare. However, the presence of the red-robed priestess alleviated any concerns one may have had.

"We have to take into consideration the size, condition, and purpose of a vessel." Richard was saying. "Too small and we will be too slow and potentially caught up by anyone in pursuit of us. Too large, the more crew we would need to detain to run it, and that doesn't include the fact that the ship's preparations would take excessively longer. We need to be in or out of here in minutes before the community rises to respond to what we're doing."

"You talk like you've done this before, Richard," said Clarissa with a tilt of her head.

"Not at all, my lady, but I am well versed in covert military tactics."

"Well, the tactic is you walk up to a blighter, stick a knife to his throat and say 'hey, we're in charge now!'" Kevin said, deliberately trying to bait the man.

"That one." Clarissa stopped walking and pointed to a small fishing vessel that could not have been manned by more than five or six people. Looking at the deck, only two appeared to be present.

"You have a good eye, my lady—a small-scale fishing vessel with a single mast," Richard said, impressed. "We should pick up some fair speed with a good wind. I take it you have experience with boats."

"Actually, Richard, I simply liked the name," Clarissa replied, pointing to the legend Lady Luck written on the side.

"Oh my, are you seriously going to steal this boat?" Sister Taylor said her eyes widened in astonishment, and a mix of fear and excitement was visible in her eyes.

"We will let you leave as soon as we are aboard," Clarissa said, not taking her eyes off the deck and the two men who appeared to be tying things down. She favored the knife in the back of her belt as she headed purposely towards the vessel. The ship was small enough that there was no gangplank, and it was merely tied up against the jetty, and a little hop-skip would have you on board the deck. The man in charge appeared older, but his large, shaggy beard hid an accurate assessment of his age. A younger man, possibly in his twenties, was working with him and appeared similar enough to the older man that they could be related. They didn't even notice as the light-weight Lady of Jilrir hit the deck, but looked up as the more heavy-footed Richard and Kevin joined her. Maddie and Taylor remained on the jetty.

"Good morning, gentlemen." Clarissa smiled.

The younger man positively beamed at the attractive woman, but the older one narrowed his eyes. "Can I be helping you, Madam?"

"We require passage to Hayburn," Clarissa stated.

"Well, I'm sorry, but we're not a passenger vessel, and we don't actually leave Heron Bay. Maybe if you..."

"Unfortunately, I'm going to be most insistent." Clarissa smiled sweetly as the crossbow slipped from her shoulder. The older man tensed, and the young man's smile dissipated.

"You're going to steal my boat?" The old man growled.

"Well, I prefer to think of it as borrowing it," Clarissa advised. "We won't keep it, we just want to get to Heyburn."

"And then you're going to bring it back, I presume." The man said sarcastically

"Well, no," Clarissa said, rather embarrassed. "We don't plan on coming back."

"So let me get this right, you're going to take my boat to Hayburn, and I'm going to have to find some way to get to Hayburn myself and pick up my boat?"

"Well, no," she flushed slightly. "You see, we don't have any sailors, and we need you to sail us up there."

The man also turned red, but in his case, it was with righteous rage. "You are aware that piracy is a capitol offence and that you will be hanged for this."

"Yes, yes, everyone wants to hang us, but can we get on, please?" Clarissa sighed.

"Clarissa, we have a problem," Maddie called out to them in an ominously singsong voice. Clarissa turned to see her pointing up the hill. The palace guards were no longer at the temple but could be seen riding down the road towards the town.

"We have to get out of here fast," Clarissa started saying, but as she turned back, she suddenly saw stars as a fist slammed into her face, and the crossbow fell from her hand. It turned out that all three of them had looked back at Maddie, and the ship's captain had closed the gap between them. Being the only one with a projectile weapon, Clarissa was his first target, but not his last. A large fishing knife was gripped in his hand, and before Clarissa had even finished staggering back from the blow, he thrust it into the side of Kevin, who went down with a shout and a cry of pain.

Richard went for the captain, but the younger man jumped upon him, his arm wrapped around Richard's neck in a headlock, trying to bring him down. Clarissa scrambled to pick up the crossbow, but with a swift kick, the captain kicked it through the entryway, and it quickly fell and sank to the bottom of the bay. She spun back to the man quickly, bringing her knee up into his groin, but she was hardly a brawler. She did manage to make contact, but not sufficiently to knock him out for the count, and he slammed his head hard into her face. She felt the cracking of the cartilage and the agony as blood ran down over her mouth.

Kevin, clutching his abdomen, crawled away from the scene, cussing and shouting and leaving a thick trail of blood. In a surprising move, Taylor suddenly jumped aboard the ship and ran over to him just as Richard managed to reverse his position and slammed the head of the young man down onto the deck. The captain stepped forward, his blade raised, ready to finish Clarissa when she suddenly pulled out her own blade and slashed it across his face. Instinctively, he stepped back and then came at her again.

"I really wouldn't do that if I were you." A low growl came.

The captain glanced over and saw Richard had the young man on the ground with his knife at his throat. Fear entered the old man's eyes, and he took a step back, raising his hands. Despite her pain, Clarissa stepped forward and reached up to take the knife out of the captain's hands. Before anything else could be said, a bright light drew their attention. All turned to see Taylor standing over Kevin, and a blue glow emanated from around her body. The look of agony on Kevin's face started to ease, and moments later, he began to stand up, but suddenly had to reach out and grab Taylor, who had fallen to her knees. There was no time to debate what was going on with the approaching palace guard.

"Get us out of here now!" Clarissa said, turning back to the captain.

"We just finished tying up for the night. It is going to take us a while to get ready to set sail."

As he spoke, Clarissa had already pulled out the puffer and was filling it with black fire powder. "It's going to take even longer if you stand around blabbing about it." As he headed off to unfold the sale, she bit off a gummed lead bullet and spat it into the spout of the weapon. She looked over Kevin. "Are you OK?"

"Yeah, to be honest, I feel damn good," he responded with surprise.

Clarissa nodded to the priestess whom Kevin had gently laid upon the deck. "How's she doing?"

"Well, she's still breathing, and she appears fine; I just can't wake her up."

Clarissa turned back to the dock and called out to Maddie. "Can you untie the moorings?"

The older woman nodded and set to work. Clarissa began to pace up and down the deck, watching the approaching horsemen as they made their way through the town, getting ever closer. They may not have even come down to the dock if it wasn't for what happened next.

The captain of a nearby boat had heard the commotion, and he was walking down the jetty with a couple of his crewmen, calling out to the captain. "Ahoy, Jenks, is everything OK?"

The captain looked like he was about to call for help, but Richard still had his son pinned down. "Everything's fine, Thompson."

The other captain looked at first as if he was going to accept that, but then he saw Richard's knee on the back of the young lad. "Fire! Foe! Murder!" The interloper screamed with the traditional cry of alarm. Up and down the docks, people started to look their way, but as Clarissa raised the puffer towards him, he and his men started to back away, eventually turning and running back down the jetty, crying out the alarm. She looked up to see the guards coming down and quickening their pace, and they were coming straight down towards the docks now. A loud flapping behind her indicated the sail was down, and the captain had to call on Kevin to help him hold down one end while he tied off the other. Then the horses of the city guard came out onto the dock, and her eyes met those of the lead rider. Shit and fuck! She knew him, but then she knew most of the palace guard, who were quite an intimate part of her previous life.

"My lady," Master Sergeant Trent called out as he slowly rode his horse to the edge of the jetty, his eyes carefully watching the firearm in her hand, which was now pointed at him.

"Good to see you again, Master Trent, although the circumstances are rather awkward right now," Clarissa called back.

"Your father will not give up looking for you, Lady Clarissa, you know this. Come back with me now before things get worse."

The boat slowly started to move, and with a running jump, Maddie came aboard and joined them, as Trent slipped off his horse. "Oh, I think things are fine just the way they are, Master Trent," Clarissa shouted back. "No. Don't come any closer, I *will* fire."

“I don’t believe you, Lady Clarissa. I have known you since you were a child, and your heart does not beat that way.” He took a few steps onto the jetty.

“Then you do not *truly* know me, Master Trent, any more than my parents do. I give you this final warning. Do not take another step.”

He hesitated momentarily, then smiled and took another step. Clarissa squeezed the trigger. There was a bang, a puff of smoke, and as it cleared, she watched him stagger back, clutching his chest and then fall to the ground. There was a twang of a quarrel that hit the deck just to the left of the Lady of Jilrir. She looks surprised at the other horsemen who had fired it.

“Hold your fire, you damn idiot.” Trent managed to gasp out. “That’s Clarissa Maine, the Second Lady of Jilrir. I really don’t think her father wants us to bring her back dead.”

“Fair you well, Trent. I am delighted I didn’t kill you, sir,” Clarissa called to him as the boat moved further and further away from the jetty. “Just remember this wasn’t personal, it was just business.”

“I will find you, Lady Clarissa,” Trent called with determination. “I won’t give up.”

Clarissa smiled and doffed the brim of the hood. “Then until we meet again, Master Trent.” She turned away and looked out across the ocean as ever so slowly Heron Bay disappeared behind them.

# Chapter Eight

## All at Sea

As the Lady Luck headed down the coastline, Lady Clarissa Maine stood at the bow looking out over the sea. To her right, the boat followed the coastline. It was far too dangerous to move outside of sight of the land, and very few ships ever did. It would only be the big war galleons that would head far out into the ocean in order to move past shorelines to surprise attack an enemy. Emily used to tell her stories as a child that there were other lands out there where people lived, but she was convinced they were nothing but a myth, for no one ever came from there, and no one ever went there. At least not a reliable source that could be believed.

Dusk was coming down, and the myriad stars started to appear. The larger of the two moons was overhead, reflecting off the softly lapping water.

"A shekel for your thoughts."

Clarissa glanced over her shoulder and smiled sweetly as Kevin approached. "How are you doing?"

"Me? I feel positively energized. I don't know what that witch did to me, but I was sure I was a goner." he pulled up his shirt, displaying the side of his abdomen. "See, there's not even a mark on me."

Clarissa's smile widened. "That wasn't witchcraft, Kevin. It was the Illyan Rite of Healing. It's not even magic. She called on the Goddess Illya to come save you, and it appears she did. Same as what that priestess did to my shoulder back in Heron Bay."

"So why won't she wake up?"

"I don't really know the details, but my understanding is that they pass on some part of their life force or something. It's not like I studied it. I just heard tales as a child."

"It's all mystical crap to me," Kevin said, but Clarissa did not reply. She stared back out over the bow and leaned against the railing. "So, where do we go, really, Clarissa? You gotta have a plan of some kind, but if not a plan, at least an idea."

"Honestly, Kev, I have no clue. I was perfectly happy in Jilrir. I had a good life, I didn't really have a problem being the Second Lady of Jilrir until they started making arrangements for my damn wedding."

"I still can't believe you would just wanna walk away from being the queen of the land. Do you have any idea of what you walked away from?"

"I absolutely do." Clarissa snorted. "And by the fact you asked me that question, I know that you don't realise what it was I walked away from."

"I thought arranged marriages were normal for you nobs."

"Oh, they are, and in principle, I don't have a problem with that. However, while I was sitting there looking at him, I realized it wouldn't work for me. I know that as queen, my entire role would be to simply provide him with an heir. If I were to marry, it would be to a man who values my counsel and respects my opinions. Crown Prince Campion barely acknowledged my existence."

"I value your opinion," Kevin said with a little hint of nervousness as he placed an arm about her shoulder. She turned to face him and found him only inches from her.

"I know you do." She smiled at him, and they stared into each other's eyes for a moment. She would never remember who initiated it, although Kevin would always claim it was her, but she found her arms around his back and him pulling her to him as they kissed. It was a rough and coarse kiss, for Kevin hadn't shaved for several days, but it was a good kiss, performed only by someone who'd cared about her. It was not like she was innocent of the ways of the world, and her parents would have completely disowned her if they were aware she was no longer a virgin. It was the simple fact that Clarissa very much enjoyed sins of the flesh, and no one preaching chastity to her was ever going to change her mind. She felt his loins pushing into her abdomen and pulled back with a smirk. "Someone's hungry for the Second Lady of Jilrir."

"I don't think I'll ever see you as that, Milady. You will always be that mysterious rogue who turned up every so often at the Calf. To be honest, I don't think I've got it wrapped around my head yet that you're a nob."

"Well, for all I know, my father has stripped me of all my titles, and I am just plain Clarissa Maine."

"Well, if he strips clear titles, technically, you will no longer be Clarissa Maine. It's unlawful for anyone outside your family to use that name."

Once more, it began to sink in to Clarissa exactly what she had done. If she had been stripped of her titles, then she truly was now the fictional persona she had pretended to be to the patrons of the Fatted Calf, playing Clarissa rogue, rebel, and mysterious traveller.

"You know, Kevin, it's going to be dangerous to hang out with me. You heard Master Sergeant Trent back there. My father is going to keep coming for me, and whilst they may well have a rule to keep me alive, they don't have a rule to keep any of you in that condition. My father is not a just man but rules with an iron fist. He would easily have you hanged, and no amount of pleading on my part will stop him."

"Well, we don't know what they know about my involvement with you. There's a big risk for me to go back now." Kevin shrugged.

"But the longer you are with me, the more that risk becomes a certainty."

Kevin simply shrugged again. "I never wanted to be an innkeeper, and with a mum who was just fourteen when I was born, it will even be a long time before I ever inherit the Calf. I may have shortened my lifespan coming with you, but it's certainly going to be more interesting than four score years mopping beer off a counter. Don't worry bout me, Clarissa, I don't regret for a moment coming with you."

She felt a warm tingling sensation in her tummy as he said this, and reaching up, she gripped the hair of the back of his head, pulled his face down to hers, kissing him hard and passionately. He responded with equal fervor. Clarissa, breathing heavily, pulled away and looked around as if to find somewhere magically private. Grabbing his hand, she led him down into the cabins.

The two crewmen had been locked in a room for the night. Both Richard and Maddie had found their own rooms, and Clarissa hoped that they were already asleep. She was supposed to be on watch, but the burning desire within her, combined with a lack of knowledge about what happens if you leave a boat unattended, drove her into the captain's room.

The room may have been a little impressive for Kevin, but it was quite basic for Clarissa, and she wasn't really paying attention to the décor. The moment the door was shut, she turned on him, pushed her body up against his own, and forced him against the wall, once more kissing him fast and feverishly as her hands reached down to unclip his braces. Her other hand groped between his legs. Nice size, she thought, comparing him to her previous lovers. He pulled off her hat and tossed it along the bed, then desperately started to undo the lace that crisscrossed her shirt down to her diaphragm. As Clarissa unfastened the final buckle, his trousers fell to his knees, and she was able to grip him, which only increased her arousal. He gasped and whimpered softly as he pulled her shirt off over her head and roughly grabbed her breasts. Clarissa rapidly released her own trousers, and both stepped out of their garments as Kevin turned her and gently lowered her down onto the captain's bed. Her knees parted, and her eyes fixed on his imploringly...

***

Two cabins down, Maddie sat up as she heard Clarissa cry out. She was about to jump out of bed to see what was wrong when she heard more cries and recognised them for what they were. A grin crossed her face as she lay back and turned to her side, and imagined what the innkeeper's son was doing to the Second Lady of Jilrir.

***

When Taylor woke up, she wondered for a moment where she was. The small cabin Kevin had placed her in on board the Lady Luck was not much different in size from her accommodation within the temple, but in terms of style and cleanliness, it was far different. It took her a while for the memory of what happened to come back to her. It had been almost instinctive for her to go to the aid of the young innkeeper's son. She had never performed the healing before. Well, not on that scale, she had occasionally helped heal the cuts and scrapes and bruised knees of the village children but that was nothing the sheer amount of energy that she had passed from herself into a lab that she wasn't sure wasn't her captor. When she suddenly became aware of the boat's motion, she sat up, startled. She looked about, but there were no portholes in the room. The ship swayed gently from port to starboard and bobbed in the current. She picked up the red robe that hung over a chair, pulled it on, and went to the door, reaching out to the handle with trepidation, wondering if she was locked in. She let out a sigh of relief as it turned out the door opened. She had no sense of time and found herself surprised to discover that it was night once she stepped out onto the deck. Although the larger of the two moons was out, its light was insufficient to see much beyond a few feet out to sea, and whether she looked port, starboard, bow, or aft, there was no sign of land. It may have eased her mind a little if she had known that, if it were daylight, it could be clearly seen on the starboard side. As she looked up at the stars, she made out the constellations.

She soon became aware that they were heading west. No, wait, they were now heading north. She continued watching the stars move in the sky and realised the boat was not going in a straight line. She had grown up in Heron Bay, the daughter of a fisherman and his wife, and was quite familiar with boats. She looked up at the aft deck and climbed the small ladder. Sure enough, the steering wheel spun clockwise, then slowed, and started moving in the other direction. She stepped up to it and turned it onto an even keel, continuing to head west, knowing that if she went south, she would sail out into the endless ocean. If they went north, they would eventually run aground.

As she maintained the ship's direction, her mind ran over all the possibilities of her situation. Should she turn the boat around and head back towards Heron Bay, there would be no point in this darkness; she would never be able to find it, and she did not know how long the boat had been sailing. She wanted to find out who was on board, but that would mean abandoning her new post, which she had taken upon herself.

"Hey, how are you doing?" Taylor visibly jumped and spun round at the voice of Clarissa Maine, who had climbed to the ladder and approached her in the darkness.

"That all depends on what you mean by how I am doing. Physically, am I fine? Yes, I am tired, but I am well. If you mean how am I doing finding out that I have been abducted aboard a boat, then not so good."

"I assure you, sister, you are not abducted." Although Clarissa chuckled lightly, she also tried to look reassuring for the young priestess. "We were under attack, and when you passed out, we could hardly toss you onto the dock when we were trying to flee. I assure you that the moment we reach port, you're free to go on your way."

"And so you intend just to abandon me in some strange town to fend for myself?" Taylor said, but there was no bitterness behind her words.

"I said you are free to go; I didn't say you *had* to go. I will not simply abandon you unless that is what you desire."

Taylor turned back to the wheel to hold it in place as it had started to move again. "You know nothing of sailing, I see."

"I grew up in Jilrir," Clarissa stated dismissively. "You can't get more of the land lover than the likes of me, but what's the problem?"

"You can't leave a boat unmanned. You are at the whimsy of the currents, and when I came out, we were drifting."

"Ah, I see. I didn't know that. I assumed the boat would just keep going straight."

"It would not continue going straight any more than a horse and cart would, in fact, it's even worse since there is no ground beneath us. If you want to go where the wind takes you, then by all means abandon the helm. Can I assume that the captain and his boy did not survive their encounter with you?"

"No, they did, but we locked him in the cabin downstairs so that we could all get some sleep."

"You don't look like you've had much sleep. I can see the weariness in your eyes."

Clarissa flushed slightly. "Well, I did get a little bit distracted."

"Well, I suggest you go and try and get some sleep now, Lady Clarissa,"

Clarissa nodded, made to turn away, but looked back. "You're not gonna try anything, are you?"

Taylor managed a smirk. "What exactly do you think I could try. Do you think that I'm going to kill you all in your sleep or jump overboard and swim in the hope of finding land? No, you're stuck with me, and I'm stuck with you... for now ... and we will see what happens when we land."

And with that, Clarissa gave a simple nod and turned away to head back towards the cabins. She did not return to the cabin she had shared with Kevin minutes before, but took another. As she reflected on her intimacy with the young man, she felt a modicum of guilt. She regretted her impulsive decision to sleep with him. Still, she had other things to worry about, for she did not know what the next day would bring. If Trent had sufficiently recovered from the wound that she had inflicted upon him, he could already be heading down the coastline, hoping to intercept her at Hayburn—no doubt they would meet again.

# Chapter Nine

# Best Little Whorehouse in Hayburn

Hayburn was the largest city in the Province of Ithia. A sprawling metropolis that spread out haphazardly across the landscape. As the primary port of the entire Southern Land, it had one of the busiest docks. The little fishing vessel, the Lady Luck, was dwarfed by the large galleons that bore two to three masts and could be crewed by up to fifty men. Clarissa and Richard stood on either side of Taylor as she navigated between these vessels towards the jetty. The noise of the dockyard grew louder as cargoes were loaded and unloaded from barriers and vessels along the Wharf. The second lady of Jilrir spoke about the commerce between the provinces and the importance of this city, but she didn't imagine the majesty. The city appeared to disappear into the horizon, but that was a false perception. Like many coastal towns, it rose in a slight gradient, and the horizon disappeared a lot sooner than elsewhere.

"We seem to be drawing a lot of attention. More than I would consider normal," said Richard, his eyes narrowed, and his brow furrowed in concern.

Clarissa came out of her thoughts and looked at the ships around them. Indeed, many of the crews were standing on the side of their ships, looking down at them; some were even shouting and waving their fists.

"What have we done wrong?" Clarissa said softly, but rolled her eyes when Richard smirked at her. "I mean, what have we done wrong that they would know about already?"

"It's simply a matter of procedure and protocol, my lady," Taylor said. "Under the King's law, all ships' passage is recorded, and the port of destination should be expecting us. Since that is not happening with us, we are being seen as a hazard to navigation for the other ships coming in and out. You should be aware that they may refuse to allow us to dock."

"Maybe you should have mentioned that earlier," Clarissa said with a sigh.

"And what would you do? Turn around and go back to Heron Bay?"

"Actually, that may be a bluff that the royal guard doesn't see coming," Kevin commented. "For I'm sure he's already on his way here if he's not here already. If we turn back, we may lose him."

Clarissa nodded thoughtfully. "I think Heron Bay militia wouldn't take kindly to us returning. Our priority must be to get off the boat and disappear into the city as soon as possible, for clearly this is the first place he would have come."

"Agreed," Richard responded as Taylor guided the boat towards an empty jetty. A man in the dark blue uniform of the Port Authority came running down, waving them back and shaking his head. He was waving his hands above his head, indicating that they shouldn't dock there. Taylor ignored him.

Clarissa watched the man as he reached the end and favored the puffer in her belt, which she had already loaded and primed. However, as she looked around the dock area, any idea of a fight was out of the question. There were literally hundreds of people moving around the port. Instead, she turned and slipped down the ladder as the priestess lined them up with the jetty. Kevin and Maddie were already waiting and watching as Clarissa made for the gangway and, with a hop, skip, and a jump, landed up on the jetty, immediately followed by Richard, and then one by one, the rest of their party, with the exception of the priestess, who would join them in a minute or two once the boat was moored.

"By Marran's beard, what do you think you're doing?" the elderly port officer was shouting and waving his hands at them as he approached. "You can't dock that vessel here. Can't you read the sign?

Being the only ones who could actually read, Clarissa and Richard looked to the wooden post that read "Orson Trading Company."

Without missing a beat, Clarissa simply smiled at him and tilted her head, saying pleasantly. "Yes, Sir, that is us."

The elderly officer looked confused, and he too tilted his head as he looked back at her. "This vessel is not on your registry."

"No, Sir, it is a recent new acquisition," Clarissa said with the irony of truth.

This seemed to confuse the man all the more as he looked at the battered old ship before turning back to her. "New?"

Clarissa chuckled politely. "Well, it's new to the company, Sir."

"It's not your typical vessel. I have never seen you use something quite so small."

"We're not here delivering cargo, Sir. May I introduce you to Lord Eugene Orson?" she indicated Richard, who looked at her momentarily, wide-eyed, before trying to assume the role of the made-up individual.

"Is this your intent to keep us here all day?" he argued in the manner of someone used to getting his own way.

This new turn of events seemed to undermine the port officer's confidence. "My apologies, but policy and protocol must be followed. You are not scheduled to be docking here today, and under the law, we are not permitted to allow it."

"Well, that is a matter you must take up with our captain, for it is his responsibility to ensure all of that is dealt with. Now, if you'll excuse me, I have business to deal with in town."

"And where is your captain?" The old man said, looking at the boat and seeing only a red-robed priestess jump onto the dock.

"I believe he is in the cabin," Clarissa said sharply, and this was no lie, for that is where the captain and his son had been locked the last two days of that journey.

And with that, Richard strode past the official. Clarissa gave a brief trot to catch up with him. The old man looked suspiciously at Kevin and Maddie as they moved past, their heads held high, which belied the status they were pretending to have. The old officer stared after them, confused and unsure of what to do.

The small party did not waste time hurrying quickly into town.

"So!" Said Clarissa wearily as they wandered with no destination in mind. "We are now in what I understand to be one of the most expensive cities in Ithia with a little more than some loose change in my purse, nowhere to go, and no one to help us."

"Oh, I think I know somewhere where you can go, but you may not like it," Maddie said with a huge grin.

Clarissa looked over her shoulder suspiciously. “Go on?”

“It’s been a few years since I was here, but I have a friend who runs a little house, or at least used to. She may not be here now, I don’t know, but it’s worth checking out if you’re interested.”

“What sort of house are you talking about, Madam?” Richard asked suspiciously, feeling certain he already knew the answer.

“A house of gentlemanly comfort,” she said, the grin widening.

“What’s that supposed to mean?” Clarissa asked, confused. Although she had spent time visiting the underbelly of Jilrir, she was not familiar with everything, and the reference was unknown to her.

“She means a whore house,” said Richard, not at all happy about the idea of taking the second Lady of Jilrir into such a place.

“Well, if you want to put it so crudely, then yes, I’m talking about a whore house,” responded Maddie. “But it’s a fairly upmarket one, at least it was back in the day.”

“It is a place that is entirely unsuitable for Lady Clarissa,” argued Kevin.

Clarissa chuckled. “Would you have said that about the Clarissa you knew a week ago. The one that you did not know was of noble birth?”

Kevin pondered this and, sinking his hands deeply into his pockets, he had to admit, “Well, no, actually I don’t think it would have been a problem then, but things are different now.”

“How so, Kevin?” Clarissa smiled, “I didn’t suddenly become made of porcelain, and whilst I admit that I’m not one to frequent a house of ill repute, I hardly think it’s going to cause me to combust into flames or shatter into a thousand pieces.”

“I must agree with the boy. Such a place is not suitable for you.” Richard stated.

"Stop calling me boy, Dick," Kevin said, unusually quite aggressively for him.

"They're more than likely to rob you blind." Richard continued, completely ignoring Kevin.

"I have nothing for them to rob," smirked Clarissa with a roll of her eyes. "And unless you have an alternative, I see no option."

"It may all be for nothing anyway." Put in Maddie. "It has been years since I've been here, and she may not be in business anymore."

"Well, there is only one way to find out. Shall we go?" said Clarissa, ending the subject.

It took Maddie some time to remember the way, as it had indeed been many years since she had been in the city. However, Richard and Kevin resigned themselves to the fact that they were taking Clarissa into a bordello, and the tensions grew once more as Maddie led them down a small dark alley. "Oh, this just gets better," said Richard, standing with his hands on his hips and shaking his head.

"Where exactly did you expect the whorehouse to be, darling? In the main street next to the jewelers?" Maddie said with a smirk.

"Come on, let's stop wasting time," Clarissa said, striding into the alley without a care in the world. Brothels were not illegal in Ithia, but they were licensed and taxed by the state. Even so, they were never in places where polite society would see them. The building in question was at the back of a milliner's, which from the main road looked just like your ordinary shop, and indeed it was, for it did indeed sell hats. However, the backrooms were more about removing clothing than putting them on, and the entrance was the back door down that dark alley. The legend over that door simply said 'Madame Teresa,' and Maddie grinned.

"The old bitch is still here. Or at least they're honouring her name." She rapped on the door, and a small slot opened. A pair of large green feminine eyes looked out. "Are you here on business or pleasure?" came back the voice, slightly muffled by the door between them.

"Hello, my dear, just tell Teresa that Madeline Arkwright is here." There was a pause, and the pair of eyes blinked; then the little slot shut, and they found themselves just waiting. A couple of minutes passed, but it seemed longer, when the door finally swung open. A large, well-built woman, almost obese, stood framed in the doorway. "Maddie darling, you look positively old." The woman looked a mix of delight and patronization.

"Terri darling, you look positively *fat*." Both women chuckled, but even the socially naïve Clarissa could tell there was some sort of tension there.

"Well, don't just stand there on the doorstep, come on in and bring your friends," Teresa said, and slowly, one by one, they went through the door, but as Taylor brought up the rear, Teresa tensed. "Have you found religion, Maddie dear?" She asked her old friend, keeping her eyes fixed on the red-robed Illyan priestess.

At this point, Clarissa had not given much more thought to the priestess and turned to look at her. "You know you don't have to come with us. You're free to go back to Heron Bay anytime you like."

Taylor simply smiled as she pulled back her hood, which was considered good manners when entering someone's home or business. "And I say to you again, Clarissa, where would I go? There is no Illyan temple in this city, and I don't exactly have the wherewithal to travel back to Heron Bay."

"Understood." Clarissa shrugged.

"She is Sister Taylor, a companion who travels with us," Maddie advised her friend. "Do not consider her to be here on some sort of holy mission to reform you."

"It is not the function of an Illyan priestess to sit in judgment of the profession in which this house represents." Said Taylor, giving a slight bow to Teresa. "Only Varga, the Goddess of Virtue, would judge you for your profession, not one such as me."

"In that case, my dear, you are most welcome." Theresa beamed, but her eyes still bore that hint of mistrust. "Come on through to the lounge."

Obviously, never having been in a whore house before, Clarissa was quite startled as they stepped through to the ornately designed room with its plush carpeting and flock walls, decked out in silver and gold, which she assumed was merely coloring, not actual valuable materials. Three women were in the room, all in their undergarments, looking quite natural as one read a book, another appeared to be writing, and another appeared to be snoozing lightly.

Teresa clapped her hands. "Come on, ladies, give me the room. I have company." Looking quite put out by the interruption, the three women simply sauntered out of a door in the back of the room as the group's hostess indicated the chairs they had vacated for them to sit in. Claressa sank into an armchair and crossed her legs. Kevin and Maddie flopped down onto a sofa, and Richard declined a seat, choosing instead to stand just behind Clarissa's left shoulder, like he was her guard. This immediately highlighted Clarissa as someone of importance and drew the attention of the brothel's madam. Whilst Clarissa's street clothes had been cut above the usual dress of average working-class individuals, the events of the past week had seen them become the worst for wear with the grime of daily activity, as well as an amount of dried blood stains. The one thing Clarissa couldn't hide without consciously thinking of it was her poise. She walked like a lady, she moved like a lady, and she even sat like a lady.

"And who do we have here, Maddie?" Teresa asked as she looked the girl up and down. "I must tell you that I am not looking for new girls at the moment."

"I say!" Richard looked most offended by this statement, and Kevin echoed the sentiment with a gasp. Clarissa flushed lightly, and Maddie laughed. "Oh, Terri, take a look at her. She would bring in double what any of your other little sluts do, but, no, all the money in Hayburn would not get Clarissa to spread her legs for coin."

"I can see that." Teresa smiled. "She's clearly someone of refinement, and not the sort of refinement that I train my girls to show to higher-standard clients. So what is it that brings you back to Hayburn? Have they run out of money in Jilrir?"

"Let's just say we're in a spot of bother with the authorities and need a place to lay our heads for a few days while we sort ourselves out," Maddie replied, failing to sound casual.

"I see," Teresa said, narrowing her eyes in suspicion, but she didn't labor the issue. "Well, I would be most happy to help, but we're not a hotel, and the number of rooms I have is limited, and they are in use both day and night. Of course, if you have the coin, I'm more than happy to put you up and ensure you are not disturbed by interested authorities."

"Had we the coin, we would stay at an inn." Maddie sighed. "I am asking for a favor."

"Oh, Maddie, you know you're very dear to me, but not enough for me that I am willing to give up substantial income to lose rooms within my establishment.. I am sorry, but I am unable to help you." The atmosphere in the room had turned decidedly cold.

Before Maddie could respond, Clarissa uncrossed her legs, crossed them the other way, folded her arms, and said. "I will find the coin you need, and I will ask for just one night to inconvenience you with our presence." Of course, it was yet another of Clarissa's impulsive statements, for she had no idea what she intended. Maddie and Kevin looked at her questioningly, and she could not see the expression of Richard shaking his head and rolling his eyes behind her.

"Indeed, and then when I see such coin, I will have rooms made up for you," Teresa said a tad curtly.

Clarissa rose to her feet. "I shall be back shortly," she glanced over her shoulder. "Richard, you're with me. The rest of you stay here."

It was the first time she spoke like it was an order, but it wouldn't be the last.

"Why can't we come with you?" asked Kevin, getting up, his voice filled with concern.

"We draw too much attention together, and we shall not be long," Clarissa advised him.

"What are you planning to do?" Richard asked as they stepped back out into the dark alley

Clarissa chuckled. "I'm not entirely sure yet. If you haven't already noticed, I'm purely winging this little adventure."

"That was a rash promise, was it not, my lady?" Richard spoke irritably as they headed out of the alleyway together. I know of no way that you can gain coin so easily."

"Richard, you keep acting like you don't know what I'm willing to do in order to survive our situation. I think you're trying to convince yourself that I'm not going to do it." Clarissa said, getting a little irritated.

Richard drew in his breath. "I genuinely don't know what you're intending, my lady, but I know it's not going to be good."

"Well, that depends on how you define good. Personally, I find not being homeless and starving to death a pretty good idea," she responded with a smirk.

"You appear to be enjoying criminality a lot more than necessary for survival." Richard sighed.

Clarissa chuckled. "I cannot deny that it doesn't get my old heart beating. There is an element of both power and risk that is most alluring, but I promise I will not put us in danger unnecessarily."

"That remains to be seen," Richard growled.

"And just what is that supposed to mean, Richard?" Clarissa narrowed her eyes.

"You appear to have a considerable amount of impulsiveness, which makes me nervous," he sighed. "You need to stop once in a while and think about your actions before performing them."

"We need coin, Richard," Clarissa replied irritably. "There is nothing impulsive about that. It is not like I can get a job. I'm not exactly trained for anything other than being a lady of refinement. Are they hiring those in Hayburn these days? Unless you want me to go back and spread my legs for a client of Madam Teresa, there is only one way to get it."

"You plan to steal it?" Richard sounded exasperated.

"Unless you have an alternative idea, Richard." Clarissa sighed. "You just need to stop being negative. Come up with solutions instead of problems, and maybe I wouldn't have to take this road. I really want to be in a position to either escape or retaliate against Master Sergeant Trent when he gets to Hayburn. Ideally, I want us to be far from here so that he loses my trail before that happens. Now, come on, I need you to have my back."

# Chapter Ten

# For a Few Sivs More

The lady and her knight headed down to the wealthier areas of the city, which were never hard to find, as they usually congregated around the center of communities. The residences around them began to look a little more upscale, featuring three-story townhouses with ornate front doors and coloured leaded windows.

She began looking around for her mark. Similar to a bodragel stalking its prey, Clarissa casually surveyed the people on the streets. She was looking for the weakest target. Someone less likely to put up resistance, but their dress indicated affluence enough that they carried a substantial amount of wealth.

"There!" Clarissa noticed an older gentleman walking with a cane, which she thought was more of a fashion accessory than a necessity, given his fair pace. Before Richard could respond, she was already crossing the road towards him, following along behind the old man, with Richard just behind her in her peripheral vision. She tried to rapidly work out a plan, as she couldn't accost a man in the middle of this public street, where she could be clearly seen. She waited until he was passing a small side road. Once again, she came up with an idea on the fly, and as he passed to the other side of the side road, she once more ordered Richard, "Wait here. Follow only when you see him come up the road with me."

She trotted into the side road and then, turning back, she called out to the old man in her finest regal voice. "Sir, Sir, can you please help me?" she said, sounding quite distressed. The old man turned around, looked her up and down momentarily. Seeing her as no possible threat, he started heading towards her.

"Whatever is the matter, my dear?" he said with a warm smile and a look of concern which gave Clarissa a modicum of guilt.

"It is my cat. He got stuck in the drain. I can't get him out. Please come help me." The old man followed her down the side road, which was when Richard was expected to follow, and reluctantly, he did.

However, her words had made the man a little bit suspicious, but not enough to stop him. "Drains? There are no drains in Hayburn other than the storm drains on the edge of the city."

When the distressed girl turned back, she was clutching her firearm. The man made to back away, but bumped into someone coming up behind and turned to see Richard. The tall man said nothing. He was incredibly uncomfortable with the entire situation.

"Sir." Clarissa gave the old man a slight smile. "My apologies for this, but my need is desperate, and I'm hoping that you can spare your purse."

There was no fear in the old man's eyes, and he looked more embarrassed that he had fallen for her trick as he reached down to his belt and started to untie his purse. Clarissa was delighted about how easy this appeared to be. He reached out to hand her the purse, but as she went to take it, it slipped from his fingers and fell to the ground. Whether this was chance or deliberate, she would never know, but without thinking, Clarissa immediately bent down to pick it up and suddenly felt the metal handle of the old man's walking stick on the back of her neck. He did not waste time and swung it round, striking it across the face of Richard before he could react.

The attack wasn't enough to incapacitate either of them, but it was enough to delay them for a second, allowing the old man to move away and start screaming for help. There was nothing they could do but run, and as Clarissa started to move away, she suddenly realised that the purse was still on the floor. Stepping back to it, she quickly snatched it up before heading down the side street at a fast pace. She kept going for several minutes before looking back to realise Richard wasn't following. She stopped to catch her breath, stared back up the street, but the twists and turns of the road meant that she couldn't see back where she'd left him. She waited about a minute, wondering whether to go back or not, but, realising that no one was following her, she was sure Richard was in some altercation. She doubled round another side street, got back onto the main road, and started heading back to Theresa's whorehouse with a throbbing, intense headache from the strike.

***

Although Richard Kyle had become frequently frustrated by Clarissa Maine's impulsiveness, it was his own impulsiveness that he regretted the most. Although born to a noble house himself, it did not hold great estates or own many miles of land. His family served as retainers to the king and his family line for several generations. He had been raised with the knowledge that one day he would serve a member of the royal family. He had achieved the second-highest position, as the Crown Prince's man; it was considered a privilege. Richard, however, did not feel that privilege. Prince Campion was not the most pleasant man to be around. Self-entitled and self-indulgent, the future king had little interest in affairs of state and concentrated most of his time on his personal pleasures. Most of Richard's roles were to hide his dalliances with various men, especially those men who would not have the same sexual persuasion, yet still had to lie with the Prince or face some form of retribution. Richard had not been happy for the longest time. However, one did not resign the position of retainer. It was a life appointment, and even attempting to do so would have been considered disloyalty at best or treason at worst.

So, when he stood outside the Fatted Calf and had to choose between helping a young woman escape from a life with the most odious man Richard knew, he had made a choice. Although he knew the consequences of his actions, he wasn't thinking about them at the time. He had responded out of concern for a young, attractive girl he found himself drawn to. In the single act of killing the guard that was trying to stop Clarissa from leaving, he had thrown his entire life away and completely reset his destiny. He had committed treason, and under the law, there was no justification for it. His life was now forever tied to that of Clarissa Maine, and her fate would ultimately be his fate.

However, as he lay upon the floor of the cobbled street in the affluent district of Hayburn, held down by men who'd come to the aid of the old man and seeing the Second Lady of Jilrir disappear around the corner, he had a modicum of regret. No one pursued her because, in the chaos, the assumption was that the man was the aggressor, and no one really paid any heed to the small slip of a girl who had been, in fact, the instigator.

City guard quickly arrived and bound Richard's hands behind his back before dragging him up to his feet. It was only when the old man had given a statement that they became aware that, apparently, a female was the instigator of this assault.

"Right," said a guard who stood in front of him as two others gripped onto his arms. "Who is your accomplice, and where do we find her?"

"I acted alone. I do not know of whom you speak," Richard said, not entirely sure why he was remaining loyal to the woman who had just left him standing there.

He doubled over as the guard slammed his fist into his stomach, winding him and causing him to double over despite the attempts of the two guards to keep him held up straight. "It will go easier on you if you tell us who your accomplice was."

"You mean I'll be spared the hangman's noose," Richard laughed dryly.

"That could be a consideration," the guard responded.

Richard was no fool, and he knew that it wouldn't be a consideration in any shape or form. The state would certainly not recognise Clarissa, a woman, as the primary instigator of the crime. The mere idea that a woman would have been in charge of such an act when a man was involved was positively ludicrous.

"I do not know her name. I paid her to be a distraction, and that is all I know." He gasped the words out, barely having the breath to speak, but it seemed to appease the guard, and he indicated for the others to take him away.

***

Clarissa cursed herself for the loss of Richard. However, it seemed there was little she could do. As she strode purposefully down the road, looking for the little alley back to the whorehouse, she examined the contents of our newly acquired purse. In one way, she had chosen her target wisely, for she now had a considerable amount of coin. It would last the average person at least a season. When she rapped on the door, the little slot slit open, then quickly closed. The door opened, letting her in.

She found the others still in the lounge, looking as though they had never moved, with the only change being the arrival of a pot of tea and some sweet cakes. "Well, I got the money, but I lost Richard," she simply blurted out as she strode to the room and threw herself down into the armchair that she had previously occupied.

"What do you mean you lost Richard?" Maddie asked.

"Literally just that. My plan didn't quite go as planned, and when it came to fleeing the scene, I thought he would have been behind me, but when I looked back, he wasn't. I'm just hoping he went in a different direction and will turn up soon."

"What exactly did you do, milady?" Kevin asked with a questioning frown.

Clarissa glanced at Theresa before saying to Kevin, "That doesn't matter. All that's important is that I have the coin." She slipped two fingers into her purse, in which she had transferred the money, and pulled out two sivs. She slid them across the small table on which the tea and cakes were set. "I trust this will cover our stay?" she said, fixing Teresa in a glare that pretty much said this is what you're getting.

Theresa simply smiled without a word and pocketed the coins. She then rose and headed to the door. "I'll see that rooms are made ready for you. I trust you don't object to sharing with Maddie, do you?"

Theresa ensured that the companions were well fed before they were shown to their rooms; however, Clarissa had remained in the lounge, waiting and hoping Richard would come. As evening drew in, clients began to turn up, and the working girls were rolled out for selection. Many had turned to Clarissa, questioning whether she was on the menu. Eventually, Teresa approached her. "You know, my dear, it really would probably be a good idea if you weren't on display in our busiest time. Can I suggest you retire to your room?"

"I understand. You have my apologies," Clarissa replied, and she was about to go to her room when, instead, she decided to go out. Both Maddie and Kevin would have certainly tried to stop her had they known she was doing this, but as she stepped out into the dark, no one knew where she was going. She wasn't entirely sure where she was going herself. She wanted to find out what happened to Richard and was only sure of one thing: he was either in a morgue or in jail.

She tried to find her way to the nearest lock-up, and it wasn't hard, as most things were clearly signposted. However, she was unsure of what to say if she were to venture inside. She paced up and down across the street from the ominous-looking building with its grey walls and ageing sign, which simply said 'Militia.' She ran over all the different scenarios in her head, but couldn't come up with something that she considered remotely believable. However, she couldn't simply go back and abandon him, if indeed he was even there, no, not after what he had done for her.

Steeling herself, she decided that she was going to do what she always did: simply wing it. As she crossed the road, her attention was drawn to a noticeboard, which made her stop and inhale sharply. Something clearly new and fresh was crudely pinned at the center of the board. Clearly, the printed image of a hand-drawn portrait of herself took precedence over the other notices. It was a reproduction of a painting of her that hung in the Great House back in Jilrir. The only relief she felt was that the image was an idealized representation of her, even though she was quite fair; it made her a ravishing beauty. Her hair was neatly tied up in braids and curls, unlike how it was now, hanging about her shoulders, dirty and unkempt, and not having been brushed in over a week.

Above it was printed the word 'Information Wanted,' and underneath were the details for reporting the person's whereabouts. Then came the image, followed by her full name, Lady Clarissa Caroline Maine. She felt fairly confident that no one could recognise her from this image, but she pulled it down all the same and stuffed it into her pocket. She looked around herself uneasily. The fact that it was there told her something that did not help her already growing stress levels.

Master Sergeant Trent was somewhere in town.

For no one else was pursuing her so swiftly that she was aware of. Fortunately, the poster did not mention any form of reward, which meant the bounty hunters would not be out looking for her. Clarissa tried to push it from her thoughts as she went up the steps to the door of the jail. It was getting late, and most of the staff had gone for the day, or only one lonely guard sat behind the desk. He looked quite bored, but that quickly changed when he looked up to see an attractive young woman coming into the building.

***

In a room behind the jail's reception area, Richard Kyle lay on an uncomfortable bunk, contemplating his misfortune. There was only one other person in the room — a man around his own age, pacing up and down in the cell next to his. For most of the afternoon, he had tried to engage that man in conversation, but no word had been forthcoming.

He responded in grunts and the occasional one-word answers. Eventually, Richard just gave up and lay back watching the time pass slowly. He did not even consider for a single moment that anyone would come to his aid. The idea that the Lady of Jilrir would possibly mount a rescue was positively ludicrous, for how could she take on the city militia and all the authority behind it?

***

On the other side of the wall, Clarrisa Maine smiled sweetly at the rough-looking militiaman who stood up, running his hands through his hair to make himself look a little bit more pleasant for the attractive young woman. Not that it was worth his time, obviously, Lady Clarissa had no interest in the dirty city guard; however, he didn't know that. She gave him her sweetest smile and approached the desk with enough of her hip swing to be alluring yet not obvious.

"Well, hello there, my name is Clarissa, and what may yours be?"

"I be Toby, Ma'am." He said breathily. "What might I be doing for you on this fine night?"

"Oh, I just had a little inquiry she said with an idea finally coming to her. "My uncle was attacked today, and his purse was stolen. I understand that you have his attacker in custody."

"That we do, ma'am. At least if it's the same man who attacked your uncle, but you can't be seeing him if that's what you want."

"No, no, I'm simply inquiring after the purse that was taken from my uncle. There was a considerable amount of coin in it, and I wanted to know if it had been returned."

"Everything he had on him is over there." He indicated the corner of the room where she instantly recognised Richard's sword and pack. "You're welcome to go look if any of his stuff is in there." The guard said little sheepishly, and Clarissa couldn't help but wonder why he was so uneasy. The truth was that, had any money been found, it would have been taken and shared among his comrades when they brought Richard in.

"Oh, I don't think that's necessary. I have everything I need right now." She smiled and glanced up behind him. "I assume that the door behind you leads to the cells?"

"Aye."

"And can I assume correctly that you are the only one with the key?"

"Aye." His eyes narrowed as he found this line of questioning becoming very suspicious. His hand instinctively went down to the sword at his belt, but no sword matched the weapon Clarissa now withdrew. The firearm from the back of her belt was now pointed squarely at his chest. "Be a dear and unlock it for me, would you, and keep your hands where I can see them."

He raised his hands in the traditional manner of surrender and slowly rose from his chair. "Be careful with that thing, girly. That's dangerous."

There was a loud bang, and the room momentarily lit up with a flash of her weapon. She was just as startled as the man who now fell dead over the back of his chair. She had not intended to fire, but she rested her finger on the trigger of the weapon; she was tense, and she had held onto that trigger a little too hard, and the weapon discharged. She stood there, weapons still pointed in his direction, her mouth wide open in shock.

# Chapter Eleven

## A Life of Crime

She immediately pulled out the pouch of powder from under her jacket, refilled the weapon, loaded it with another gummed ball, and slotted it back into her belt at the back. She stepped around the table and looked down at the man who stared up at her with vacant eyes before reaching down and pulling a large key ring from his belt. She had to try several keys before the door unlocked, and she stepped through. The two occupants behind their cells were already standing, gripping the bars to see who was coming in. There was no lighting in the room. They could only make out her silhouette before she turned back, grabbed the lantern from the desk, and stepped in once more.

"Clarissa!" Richard Kyle looked at her in astonishment as a mix of confusion and relief washed over him.

She placed the lantern on the floor and fumbled with the keys, trying several before the door to the cell swung open. Before she could stop herself, she threw her arms around Richard, hugged him tightly, and kissed him on the cheek. He actually found himself laughing despite the lack of amusement in their situation. "Good to see you too, my lady."

"I thought I lost you for good."

She turned back toward the door when the man in the other cell called out to her in a rough lower-class dialect. "Hey, what about me?"

She looked back at him as Richard picked up the lantern. "What about you?"

"If you let me out, too. I'll make it worth your while." He said hopefully.

"What are you in for?" Clarissa asked.

"Does it matter?" he frowned.

Clarissa shrugged, "I suppose it doesn't, but for what reason should I let you out?"

"I'm Lincoln Granger, otherwise known simply as Lynk. I'm sure you've heard of me." He looked surprised.

"I'm sorry, but I haven't, but then I'm not from Hayburn," Clarissa responded.

"No, I can hear that in your voice. You sound like a toff, but your dialect is distinctly Jilririan."

"Make your case fast, Sir, as I don't think we should be tarrying here," she said impatiently.

"I'm a lieutenant in the Tallymen, and if you let me out, the Tallymen will owe you a favour, and a Tallymen favour is worth more than gold."

"The Tallymen?"

"It's a criminal syndicate, my lady," Richard said, not hiding his contempt. "Smuggling, racketeering, prostitution, slave trading... You name it, they have their filthy little hands in it."

Lincoln smiled, revealing two missing front teeth. "Don't get overly judgmental on me because if I'm not mistaken, that sound was either a carbine or puffer going off, and by the fact she is standing there with her back to the door, I assume a little guard out there is worm food."

"I assure you, it was an accident." Clarissa protested casually. "My weapon went off unbidden by me."

"Look, we can stand here and chew the fat, or we can get out because they don't exactly leave just one guard sitting here. Next door, at least half a dozen other militia are getting their kip, and they will have heard your little interaction. Come on, let me out. I can help you, and you don't really wanna turn your nose up at that in your position."

"My position?"

"You just killed a militiaman. When they catch up with you, you won't survive long enough to be hanged. You're more likely to meet with a very unfortunate and very violent accident before you face the beak. Now, if you're new here to Hayburn and haven't heard of the Tallymen, I assume you don't have any friends. I want to be your friend. Come on. Let me out."

"I strongly advise against it, my lady," said Richard, who sighed as she slotted the key into Lincoln's cell door. "So, of course, you completely ignore me again," he muttered.

Lincoln stepped out of his cell with a huge grin upon his face and had the audacity to pat Clarissa on the cheek. "There's a good girl. Come on, let's get the fuck out of here." Clarissa found herself following the disheveled man out of the door. She was halfway down the street with him before she looked back to see Richard, a bit of a distance behind them, half running, half walking, trying to catch up. "Come on! We can't hang around."

"I had to get my stuff," he said, indicating his sword and pack.

"We need to take a different direction, Mr. Lincoln," Clarissa said as they reached a crossroads, and it appeared that Link was going straight across.

The ruffian stopped and turned back to her. "Meet me tomorrow night in the Iron Rod, it's a tavern on Square Street, and we could discuss payments of our favor."

"Oh, I don't think that will be necessary, Sir." Clarissa smiled.

"The Tallymen pays its debts, my dear. It is a matter of honor."

"Honor from the Tallymen?" Richard chuckled. "Now there's an oxymoron if ever I've heard one." Lincoln shot him a glare, not even remotely amused by the officer's quip. Clarissa elbowed her companion gently.

"If you insist, Sir, I will be there, but for now, fair you well." Without another word, Clarissa turned east and hurried up the road at a brisk pace.

***

It was the early hours of the morning when Clarissa and Richard made it back to Teresa's little whorehouse, and business had begun to quieten down. Most of the clients were leaving rather than arriving and paid little heed to the couple that flopped down on the sofa in the lounge. Clarissa rubbed her eyes. She let out a long, unladylike yawn. "It's funny how exhaustion hits you only after the heart stops pounding."

"While you should certainly get some sleep, we need to be back on the road tomorrow," Richard advised. "You killed a militiaman, and everyone is going to be out hunting for you."

"Maybe that's the favor I can ask of Lincoln. To get us transport to Regor." Clarissa responded sleepily.

"Be careful embroiling yourself in the machinations of the Tallymen. They are considerably powerful and considerably ruthless."

"Well, I hardly consider asking for a ride to Regor as signing up to a criminal syndicate, Richard, but I'll heed your counsel and be careful. However, for now, I am going to bed." Without another word, Clarissa rose and headed off to the room that she was to share with Maddie, who was fast asleep and snoring lightly as she stripped off her clothes and climbed into bed.

Despite her exhaustion, she struggled to fall asleep. Her mind was racing with everything that had happened and pondering what was to come. She had gone through her life where the biggest crisis was how to get out of doing needlepoint classes, to having killed three men. She felt some guilt at this, but was more concerned that she did not think she felt guilty enough. She had once heard that it gets easier after the first time, and although she did not believe it at the time, she did now. It was almost dawn before she finally drifted off. She slept for most of the next day. No one disturbed her, and it was late afternoon once she finally got up. Her companions had spent most of the day getting in the way of Madame Teresa's business, and she was not in an overly pleasant mood. However, she chose not to engage.

It turned out that her companions had already learned of the activities from the night before from Richard. Kevin immediately protested about her going out alone, but she simply ignored him. "I'm going to meet with Lincoln tonight and see if he can get us passage to Regor. We can't stay here."

"Surely a few days would be fine," Maddie queried.

Clarissa pulled out the wanted pamphlet from her pocket and tossed it onto the occasional table in front of her. Maddie just looked at it and shrugged.

"That vaguely looks like you, but not enough that you could be recognized."

"I agree, but it does mean that someone from Jilrir got here ahead of us and is looking for me."

"That and the jailbreak last night, the militia will be hunting us down." Put in Richard.

"You said there were no witnesses, at least none that survived other than this Lincoln fellow, so they will not be looking for Clarissa and will probably put it down to a Tallymen action."

"There is the consideration that this Lincoln will eventually realize that he has met Lady Clarissa Maine," said Richard. "And no doubt the longer we evade authority, a reward will be offered, probably a substantial one that would tempt even a virtuous man, and I'm fairly certain that Lincoln is not virtuous."

"Well, I'm sure to find out his intentions tonight when I meet with him."

"I once more protest your idea that you should be involved with such lowlife fellows," Richard said earnestly.

Clarissa reached the end of her patience. "You know something, Richard, you're always coming up with problems, doubts, and protests, yet *never* solutions. Now we have enough coin to be able to hire or even buy a cart to get us to Regor, but that will involve us engaging with potential witnesses to our presence. Lincoln may be able to get us out without any of that bother."

"Milady," Richard responded with equal aggression. "The Tallymen is one of the most ruthless organizations throughout the land. It has its filthy little fingers in every pie, and try as it might, the state has never been able to get control of the situation. Murder, kidnap, extortion, blackmail, racketeering, prostitution."

"It is not like we have a lot of friends to help us, Richard," Clarissa shouted back. "We could go hire a cart or wagon from a legitimate source, but that leaves witnesses who know we were there. I'm fairly certain that my father's men would have already visited all methods of transportation that would get us out of here. Trent knows we're here, and we need to ensure that the trail goes cold. Does that make sense?"

"Unfortunately, it does, my lady," Richard said with a resigned sigh and sat back.

"Kevin and I will go there this evening and see the lie of the land. If things don't work out, then fine! We'll find an alternative, but right now I have no alternative."

"You will not permit me to come with you?" Richard looked offended.

"You have already shown yourself to be antagonistic towards Lincoln, and you can see in his eyes that he does not like you. Additionally, Kevin is more naturally attuned to the kind of people we are likely to meet."

Kevin smirked. "What you're saying is, milady, as a working-class peasant, I'll fit in better."

Clarissa flushed slightly. "Not how I would have put it, Kevin, but yeah, that's the gist of it."

***

As it turned out, the Iron Rod turned out to be a more upmarket establishment than either Clarissa or Kevin would have imagined. However, it made sense, as Clarissa would consider later. An untouchable criminal gang would certainly have a substantial amount of coin.

As she stepped inside and saw the patrons, she realized that maybe Richard would have been a better fit than the scruffy-looking Kevin who came in behind. At first, it seemed an ordinary establishment with a middle-class clientele drinking, laughing, and making merry, yet in a more dignified way than they would in the Fatted Calf. There was no dancing on tables, and no fiddlers played. However, she quickly noticed that they were being watched by various individuals who stood alone around the bar, without a drink, simply surveying everyone within. The two strangers immediately drew their attention, and their eyes never left them as they made their way up to the bar. A pleasant young serving wench came up to them with a smile to take their order. "I'm here to see Lincoln," Clarissa said pleasantly.

The serving girls smiled and dropped immediately. "I don't know anyone by that name, Misses," she said uneasily, clearly lying.

"I assure you he is expecting me," Clarissa said, realizing the man who had just escaped jail was hardly going to make himself public.

"It's alright, Tiffy. I'll take care of this." A tall, bull-shouldered man approached. One that had clearly seen his fair share of violence if the scars on his face and arms were anything to go by.

"Mr. Lincoln is expecting you," he said, his voice becoming quite pleasant although he did not smile as he addressed the Second Lady of Jilrir.

"And you know who I am?" Clarissa responded with surprise

"You clearly fit the description of the individual that Mister Lincoln is expecting."

"Do I really stand out that much?"

"Well, let's just say women don't generally come into the Iron Rod and ask to speak to Mr. Lincoln. Please follow me."

He led them out to the back of the bar and through the back door. A group of four more men was seated at the table, playing cards. They stopped to look up; however, seeing Clarissa's new companion, they relaxed, giving him a nod of acknowledgement before returning to their game. Clarissa followed the man around the gaming table and to another back door.

Lincoln was not alone when they entered a gaudy yet affluent-looking office with high-quality furniture that didn't match. It seemed they had chosen it purely for its value rather than its aesthetic qualities, a typical example of lower-class people coming into money. Lincoln was seated in an armchair as a scantily clad woman massaged his shoulders. He was moaning softly, but suddenly stopped and opened his eyes to look at Clarissa and Kevin as they came in. He instantly waved a hand in the air, dismissing the masseuse, who, without a word, stepped past them and went out the door. Their escort followed her and closed the door behind him.

"Come in, come in, take a seat," Lincoln said, getting up and clearly pleased to see her. "I admit I had doubts that you would come."

"I realized that I could do with that favor you offered," Clarissa said, sitting back in the chair opposite, as Kevin took the seat next to her.

"This is Kevin, an associate of mine. Kevin, this is Mr. Lincoln."

"Nice to meet you, Kevin."

"Likewise, Mr. Lincoln," Kevin said, shaking his hand.

"Oh, let's skip the formalities, shall we? Please call me Link," he said as he stepped over to a small bar. "Can I get you something to drink?"

Clarissa's eyes alighted upon a bottle on the counter, and a slight smirk crossed her face. "Is that Portillo Brandy that I see?"

"Indeed, would you like a glass?" Link chuckled.

"Considering that Portillo Brandy is distilled exclusively for the consumption by the House of Maine. That is really a rare treat."

"It does not come cheap. Probably one of the most expensive liquors on the black market. However, nothing is impossible to obtain if you work hard enough." He handed her a glass and another to Kevin, who, although he ran a Tavern, had never had a brandy before, let alone one of the best in the land.

Link returned to his seat with a glass of his own and, crossing his legs, studied Clarissa carefully. "So, tell me, how can I be of service to you and repay you for the service you have done me this day?"

"We need to get to Regor."

Lincoln laughed. "Simple enough. You don't need me to help you with that."

"We need to get to Regor without anyone else knowing, especially anyone official."

"Ah, but that's the real trick, isn't it?" Link chuckled. "So tell me why it is you need such secrecy?"

"Now that is a strange question," Clarissa smirked.

"How so seems perfectly reasonable to me." Link frowned.

"Does it indeed? You are perfectly aware that we have just liberated one of my colleagues from jail. I, therefore, would be pursued, yet you think there was more to it than that?"

"Oh, I know there is more to it than that," Lincoln smirked back. "I just wanted to see if you were willing to tell me."

"Oh, you're expecting trust from someone you just met after revealing that you are some sort of Lieutenant within the Tallymen?"

"I understand that trust is earned, so I'm going to be totally open and honest with you." Lincoln smiled. "One of the reasons that I am able to sit here is that my escape from jail is not a priority for the militia. They have been given another task, and that task is to find Lady Clarissa Maine, the Second Lady of Jilrir, for she has apparently run away from her family."

"And what exactly do you think that has to do with me?" Clarissa replied, trying to sound nonchalant.

"Oh, come now." Lincoln chuckled. "You may dress like a regular person, but anyone can see that your clothing is stitched to the highest standard. You look more like a rich girl playing a peasant in a pantomime who couldn't quite bring herself to wear something made for the lower classes. You are Lady Clarissa Maine, Second Lady of Jilrir, daughter of the baron. Currently, the most sought-after individual in the province."

Kevin tensed, and Lincoln clearly saw it. He raised her hand. "Relax, I'm not about to turn you in. I'm far too intrigued."

"Can you help us?" Clarissa said after a long pause that hung in the air.

Another pause as Lincoln pondered. "I can, but I have a proposition for you."

"I'm listening."

"I do not know why you are on the run from your family, but I am assuming that you don't exactly have access to the family treasury and are in need of money. I can not only get you to Regor, but I could make it financially worth your while to."

"I'm still listening," Clarissa said, intrigued.

"I will supply you with a wagon and horses that will get you to your destination, but I asked you to carry with you a cargo of goods. Upon delivering this cargo, you will be paid eight hundred sivs."

Kevin gasped, for this was a fortune for someone like himself. "What is the cargo?"

Linc shrugged, "The usual stuff, liquor, beer, weed, and weapons."

"Basically, anything that there's a high sales tax upon?" Clarissa realized.

"Exactly, my lady, and if you get caught, there will be no repercussions because of who you are. The House of Maine is the tax collector, and you can't be accused of evading paying yourself."

"Oh, don't be too sure of that, Link. My father is not exactly a lenient man, even with his own progeny. However, the money you are offering sounds good to me. I think we can do a deal."

"Milady." Kevin started to protest, but was quickly silenced by her raised hand in his direction.

"Can you be ready for us to depart on the morrow?" Clarissa smiled.

"I think we can surely arrange that, my lady." Linc smiled.

# Chapter Twelve

## On the Road

It was a foggy dawn, unusual for the time of year, when Clarissa's group of companions bade farewell to the best little whorehouse in Hayburn.

They met on the northern side of the city, in what was known as the warehouse district. Goods came into the city either by the ports, then took to the road with supplies throughout Ithia.

Most of the warehouses were owned by the big merchant princes. However, the warehouse where Clarissa met Lincoln once more was called Smothers and Son. There was no such person as Smothers, and it was simply a cover for the operations of the Tallymen. Whilst officers of Customs and Excise oversaw the whole region, they obviously steered clear of this particular warehouse. No doubt, the Tallymen was paying off people in the right places.

The small group did not enter the warehouse itself; the two wagons were prepped and ready in the forecourt, each led by two horses. Each wagon was laden with goods that couldn't be seen as they were covered by large tarpaulins that would be tied down around the sides.

The warehouse workers who came and went around the area did not look out of place, given that they worked for a criminal syndicate, and everything seemed to be a perfectly legitimate operation.

Lincoln met them at the gate, authorising their entry, but with him was the large scarred man who had introduced them the previous day. "Good morning, Lady Clarissa, and welcome to your first day as a member of the Tallymen."

Clarissa smiled. "Well, I'm not quite ready to go that far, Mr. Lincoln. Let's just call ourselves partners."

Lincoln chuckled, "As you wish, my lady. Although let's be careful that partners don't end up becoming rivals."

"Oh, I assure you I'm in this for survival and have no intention of pursuing a criminal career. No, we intend to just get to Regor and disappear."

"I understand your intentions, but as much as you wish to escape the House of Maine, you're going to find it very hard to escape in the comforts of a wealthy woman," Linc smirked. "You're going to find it a harder life out there than you can possibly imagine, especially as a single woman."

"I understand, and I'll cross that bridge when I come to it. Can we get on with this, please?"

"As you wish, my lady. When you arrive at Regor, you want to take your cargo to the Blue Bore Tavern. You'll meet a man named Blake, who will ensure that the goods are taken off your hands and that you receive the agreed-upon payment. You will then have the option of being introduced to The Master."

"That's nice. And just who is this master?"

"He is the head of the Tallymen operations, and if you choose to, he will discuss a position for you within the organization, but honestly, there will be no hard feelings if you choose not to meet with him."

Clarissa nodded thoughtfully. "I will consider your suggestion as we travel to the city."

"Um, hey!" Their attention was drawn by Kevin, who was lifting the tarp on a wagon and looking inside. He gripped a puffer weapon. "Can I have this?"

Lincoln smiled. "You can buy one, and I'll even give it to you with the Tallymen family discount."

Clarissa stepped over to look under the tarp as well. There were stacks of handguns and long ones known as carbines. "Can we purchase more than one?"

"Absolutely. They are, after all, being taken to Regor to be sold. Where the money comes from doesn't really bother me." Link chuckled.

She pulled out a long carbine and tossed it to Richard. "Do you know how to use one of these?"

"I have an understanding of how they work," Richard replied. "And I fired one once or twice, but never used it in combat."

"Good enough for me." Clarissa then looked towards Maddie, who nodded, and another carbine was thrown over to her. The Second Lady then took out another puffer and slipped it into her belt opposite the one she already had. "OK, two carbines and two puffers. What do I owe you?"

"Oh, settle up with Blake when you get there; it can be deducted from your fee." Link waved a hand dismissively. "All inventory has to be accounted for by the Regor branch. Paperwork is such a bitch."

Clarissa's eyes alighted on the Illyan priestess. Taylor had dispensed with her Illyan robes and was now dressed in hard-wearing traveling clothes, including leather pants, a linen shirt, and boots, in order not to stand out as much. "Are you sure you still want to come with us?"

"I must admit I'm of two minds." Taylor said softly. "Embarking on a life of criminal activity is not exactly the destiny of an Illyan priestess, yet I am intrigued about how this all plays out. I am already answerable to my Esselar for the part I've played so far, and my days as a priestess may be numbered already. So to be honest, I have nothing to lose but to continue with you."

"Excuse me?" Lincoln's eyes narrowed. "Did I understand correctly, but this woman is a priestess of Illya??"

"You did, Mr. Lincoln. Is that a problem for you?" Clarissa narrowed her eyes at him.

"It possibly is my dear lady. The Goddess of Justice is hardly a friend to the Tallymen." Link replied.

"Nor are we enemies of the Tallymen, Mr. Lincoln," Sister Taylor said solemnly. "There is a common misconception that law and justice are interchangeable terms. Many laws can be unjust, and justice can often conflict with established societal norms. Illya views justice as being about fairness, rather than legality. Even when it comes to crimes like theft and murder, there could be justice in them. A starving person may be compelled to steal food, and it is only unjust if they could afford to purchase that food and their circumstances are such that they cannot pay for it. A person suffering abuse from another that they cannot escape could justifiably murder that person in the eyes of Illya. So don't judge me as being on the Tallymen's side or against it. I do not look at organizations, I look at individuals."

Linc narrowed his eyes, his voice uneasy. "Your Esselar has often spoken out against us."

"I am not aware of that, but even if she did, she would be speaking out against such actions your organization takes, not to the organization itself. Inherently, we do not take sides. Justice is blind."

"I hear your words, Sister. Yet, I am still not happy about this, and I say to you, Lady Clarissa, if you take her with you, you will be responsible for her actions." Link said forcefully.

"You do know that I'm not actually the leader of this group, and everyone here does whatever they do willingly." Clarissa said irritably.

Lincoln laughed. "Whether you choose to or not, you are the leader of this group, and no one disputes it." Both Clarissa and Lincoln looked around at the group, and no one disagreed with his assessment.

Clarissa sighed as she realised she was indeed the leader of this group. She was the one common connection between all but the priestess. She had been raised in a leadership role, not quite the same as her brother, who would lead a province, but she would have been expected to lead a household, and her authority over those around her prepared her for such a role. However, the one thing she was trying to escape was responsibility. As they prepared to leave, it weighed heavily on her mind.

"OK, so I'm going to go into the lead wagon, and Kevin can come up with me. Richard and Maddie take the next, and Taylor, you can go wherever you like."

"I think it's better if I go in front with you," Richard said firmly, stepping forward.

"OK, can you drive a wagon?"

Richard flushed lightly. "Well, no, I've never needed to, but it can't be that hard."

"Well, we don't have time for driving lessons, and I don't know how to drive a wagon, either. Kevin does, and so does Maddie; therefore, it makes sense for me to go with Kevin and for you to go with Maddie. That is, unless you want us women folk to go ahead."

Richard sighed, "I see your point, my lady."

So it was a very smug-looking Kevin who kept smirking at Richard as he climbed up into the wagon. Clarissa sat beside him and loaded her second puffer as the two wagons started to pull out of the gate. She took Kevin's weapon and primed it to.

***

It was a single straight road that took them to Regor. Apart from the occasional twist and turn around some terrain. It was better maintained than most, since it was an essential artery of trade and commerce. The cobbles were of the finest quality and wide enough for two wagons or carts to pass each other without the awkwardness of going off-road.

They were actually heading back toward Jilrir; this would be the very road anyone from that city would take to Hayburn. Being aware of this, Clarissa remained alert for anything or anyone that looked official. Just in case her father sent out more than Trent to pursue her, which he most likely had. She also had to watch out for what was coming up behind her, for men riding horseback moved faster than wagons. They did not meet anyone often, but it would be a two-day drive to the city. With no one in the company even remotely experienced in merchant trading, no one knew exactly the protocol for meeting others while in transit. Not only did they need to be wary of those pursuing the second lady of Jilrir, but they also had to be alert for potential signs of highwaymen.

With the ultimate penalty for highway robbery being a long drop from a short rope, there was nothing for highwaymen to lose by killing everyone in the party.

"You're very quiet, milady," Kevin said as he drove the cart. At his side, Clarissa slouched down in her seat, her legs stretched out and crossed at the ankles, her arms folded, and her hat pulled down low over her eyes to avoid the morning sun's rays.

"I'm just wondering about where we go from here."

"North," Kevin replied simply.

Clarissa lifted the brim of her hood and looked up at him questioningly. "Why north?"

"Well, east is back to Jilrir. South is back to Hayburn and the sea. West is the Impassable Mountings. So if you want to put as much distance between you and your father, then the north is the only option.

"You do know the Impassable Mountains are not really impassable." Clarissa grinned. "They're just named that because they go from sea to sea without a break, but there are paths through them, and you can get boats from Hayburn, or at the great lakes to cross, and west can take us much, much further away."

"Maybe so, but I hear there are barbarian lands over there."

Again, Clarissa was amused at her companion's lack of education. "The capitol city of Aranar is west of the mountains. For sure, the further west you go, there are some let's say rural communities and even some communities that don't come under the rule of the king, but far from barbarian."

"Have you been there, milady?"

"No, I have never been further from Jilrir than the Nethili Outpost or Ternal. At least not until now."

"Then with all due respect, milady, you don't know any more than I do about what lies west."

"I have never seen a bodradgel, yet I know they exist." Clarissa grinned.

"Really?" Kevin smirked. "Have you ever met anyone who's actually seen one?"

"Well, no. No one encounters a bodragel and survives." Clarissa said it like it was obvious.

It was Kevin's turn to chuckle patronisingly. "You do realise that makes absolutely no sense. If no one survives, how could we possibly know about their existence?"

"What do you mean?"

"It stands to reason, milady. Anyone who's described a bodragel or even given it the name would have had to survive in order to do so."

Clarissa chuckled. "You raise a fair point. However, people have seen the other side of the mountains and reported what they're like, as there are people who live there. I even have cousins over there, for nearly all the great houses are related." Kevin looked out across the plains, clearly something on his mind. "OK, what's bothering you?" Clarissa asked.

"Back in the Calf. What were you doing?"

"What do you mean?" Clarissa frowned.

"What was a nob like you doing coming down to the Calf. The likes of you don't hang out with the likes of us."

Clarissa sighed. "It was just a bit of fun, Kevin. Life as a lady of Jilrir is not exactly all it's cracked up to be."

Kevin laughed. "Most people in the Calf would kill to be in your position."

"Only because they don't know what it's really like, especially for a woman." Clarissa snorted.

"Yeah, but you had safety and security, and you gave that up," Kevin said, trying yet failing to understand her motives.

"Yep, I did indeed have that, but what's the point in being safe and secure if that's only gonna make you miserable. I'd rather take the risk of this life over the one I left behind."

"So you consider yourself happy now?" Kevin responded disbelievingly.

Clarissa pondered this, sitting back again and folding her arms. "Well, no. At least not until I know what lies in my future." Then a wide grin crossed her face. "But you know what?" She gently elbowed Kevin in the ribs. "It's certainly going to be fun finding out."

# Chapter Thirteen

## *Stabbed in the Back*

The green plains disappeared behind them as they continued their journey for a few hours. The ground grew hillier, and the gradient began to steepen, forcing them to slow as the strain on the horses increased. Eventually, they began descending into a small valley, and as dusk approached, they took the wagons off the road and camped for the night. Clarissa watched carefully as Kevin took some firewood out of the back of the wagon and started a small fire, something she had never done before or even seen, for that matter. There was no need for campfires in the city of Jilrir.

"We need to set up a standing watch. The boy and I should take turns," Richard said as Maddie unpacked their provisions and started to prepare some food for cooking.

"Would you stop calling me boy?" Kevin said quite aggressively.

"We should all take turns and keep watch," said Clarissa, although if she were honest with herself, she would have just liked to lie down and sleep then and there. "I really don't think it would be wise to have Kevin driving on only half a night's sleep."

Taking this as a personal slight against his abilities, Kevin turned on the second lady with some annoyance. "I could manage quite well, milady. I don't need special treatment."

"Fine!" Clarissa said irritably, taken aback by his aggressive stance. "The two men can take the watch."

Settling down to fresh bacon and grits, Richard asked something that was on everybody's mind. "Have you given any more thought to your intentions once we arrive in Regor, Lady Clarissa?"

Clarissa pondered her answer to this, for she had indeed thought of little else. "I think the priority should be to get us as far away from Jilrir as possible. We need to lie low and not draw attention to ourselves. I want to go west, but Kevin wants us to go north."

"To go west, we would need to cross the mountains," said Richard. "There are only two ports within a reasonable distance to take a sea route. We already know that your father has Heyburn covered, and I do not doubt that he has the great lakes port covered as well. There's a way known as the High Pass, but it's just west of the Nethili Outpost. It is a treacherous route for those without extensive wilderness experience."

"But that is also a good reason for us to go that way," Clarissa said as she lay back on her bedroll and turned on her side to face them. "For I'm confident my father's people do not think that I have either the wherewithal to take such a path."

"No." Richard laughed quite patronizingly. "He would not consider you to be so foolish as to take that route. It is foolhardy and dangerous, and I must agree with the boy."

"*Stop* calling me boy," Kevin snapped.

"There is an alternative," Maddie said, drawing the attention of the others. "We could talk to that Master. It's all well and good going north or west or east or south, but survival requires money, and whilst you had a fair take back in Hayburn and more to come in regor that will not last for all of us."

"Are you really suggesting that the Second Lady of Jilrir embroils herself even further with a criminal syndicate?" Said Richard incredulously

"Isn't it being the Second Lady of Jilrir that Clarissa is trying to escape from?" Maddie scoffed. "A time will certainly come when her father considers her to be lost or even dead."

Clarissa was not sure that she liked the idea, even though, as she discussed it, that was exactly what she had been hoping for. To be left alone and to be considered dead by her family. She thought of Clarence and how he would grieve for her, and there was a hole in her heart as she realized there was a possibility she would never see him again.

"They will no doubt place a bounty upon her head," Richard continued. "At least for information, for it won't be wanted dead or alive. That is the one advantage you have, milady. You are not being hunted for your crimes, but for your status."

"And that is one of the reasons I remain," said Taylor. "For there is no justice in this. You should have the right to abdicate your titles."

"It is already irrelevant now." Clarissa shrugged it off. "I have humiliated the Prince, and any concept of a marriage with him is null and void."

"Then what is the stop here returning to Jilrir?" Kevin asked.

"My insult to the crown prince may eventually be forgiven, although I doubt it, but I am still a commodity in the political game. I will be married to someone, but now I will be considered damaged goods, and it will be to a lesser house under the lesser individual, and my life, all the same, will not be mine."

"You live in a different world." Kevin shook his head thoughtfully.

"Not anymore, Kevin." Clarissa paused, and turning onto her back, she stared up at the stars and the twin moons with a yawn. "Anyway, we can decide this in the morning. I need to get some sleep."

The bedrolls were thin, hay-filled mattresses, and nothing like what Clarissa was used to with her soft, well-sprung mattress, which was back at the great house in Jilrir. Although she had slept under the stars several times before, she found it uncomfortable and difficult to sleep. She lay looking up at the stars. One by one, the company drifted off. The only sound was the cicadas, and one of the company members softly snoring, but she couldn't tell who. The only other person awake was Kevin, who sat on watch some distance away toward the road. She didn't know how much time had passed. It seemed to be an eternity before she finally started to drift off, but as she turned onto her side, any thought of sleep suddenly disappeared as Kevin cried out, "Hey, stop there."

Clarissa was quickly on her feet, grabbing up the two puffers that she had laid down beside her. There was a loud bang from a firearm, and she saw a brief flash illuminate the area, allowing her to make out Kevin looking towards two shadowy figures in the distance. She ran up beside him. She saw the figures running off into the darkness, but she was quickly distracted by the cries of a man lying on the floor by one of the wagons.

"They were trying to take one of the wagons," Kevin informed with a low growl. Clarissa stepped over to the man lying upon the floor, clutching his shoulder and crying in pain.

The disheveled, greasy-haired man looked up at her with disdain and spat. It didn't even reach her, but instinctively, she took a step back with a disgusted look crossing her face. "What a thoroughly unpleasant individual." She lifted her boot, placed it up on his chest, and pushed him back down from his elbow until he lay on his back. This caused the pain to increase, and his screams rent the air.

"Stay here," Richard said as he approached with his carbine in hand. "There may be no honor among thieves, but his companions *may* come back." He started heading in the direction the two others had gone.

Kevin looked up at Clarissa. "Are you OK here with him?"

"My friend here isn't going to be a particular problem," Clarissa said, pointing the puffer at the man's head.

Kevin nodded, then trotted to catch up with Richard. Maddie had lit a lantern and now approached, and Clarissa's eyes alighted upon the familiar face of the scarred man who was the security for Lincoln and the Tallymen.

"Well, this is certainly a funny turn of events." Her eyes narrowed. "Why the hell is the Tallymen trying to steal their own cargo?"

"I've got nothing to say," the man growled, wincing through his agony as the blood began to run between his fingers. Clarissa looked to her friend, trying to make sense of it, but Maddie just looked back and shrugged. Having grown up in a household where she could frequently hear the enemies of her father being tortured down in the dungeons, Clarissa did not have a lot of empathy when she lifted her boot again and placed it down on the wound on his shoulder. He cried out in pain and tried in vain to grab her ankle. She raised the weapon to his face.

"Oh, I think you do have something to say," she said, pressing her boot down hard on his fingers until he managed to pull them away. This only helped her come into direct contact with where the lead ball had entered his shoulder. “Why is the Tallymen stealing their own cargo?”

“Because you’re Lady Clarissa.” He gasped out in pain, and Clarissa lifted the pressure as a reward for answering his question. “That makes no sense. Kindly elaborate.”

“If you arrive in Regor without the cargo, you will be expected to compensate the Tallymen for the loss. You would be compelled to work for us.”

“We’re hardly experienced criminals, my friend. Why would he go to so much trouble?”

“Because you are Lady Clarissa.”

“Yes, yes, you’ve already said that, but what has my being Lady Clarissa got to do with anything?”

“You are immune from the law. A very powerful position to be in. The Tallymen thinks that it would be incredibly useful to its business plans.” He gasped out.

“But I already told you that I would consider his proposal.” Clarissa was confused.

“He just wanted to make sure that you made the right decision.”

“Well, he’s not exactly winning me over right now.” She looked up suddenly as she heard the sound of weapons fire in the distance. Two shots, then a third, and far too quickly in succession for either Richard or Kevin to have reloaded. At least one shot had been at them. “Is that all you have to tell me?” she asked urgently.

“It’s all I know.” His voice was now a pained hiss.

“Thank you.” She raised the puffer to his face and fired. His face blossomed into a crimson flower of blood. He twitched momentarily, then lay still, but Clarissa was already reloading. The old saying was right. It did get easier the more you kill. “You two stay here. I’m gonna see if Richard and Kevin are OK.”

"Yeah, yeah, whatever," said Maddie as she primed her carbine and followed.

"I guess I will stay here and give this man his last rites." Taylor sighed, not too pleased by the Second Lady's actions. However, Clarissa wasn't even paying attention as she strode down the road in the direction of the weapons fire. Another shot rang out, and Clarissa quickened her pace, following the flash of light she could see in the distance. She let out a sigh of relief as she saw Richard and Kevin standing over the two dead bodies of the scarred man's companions.

"We'd best get them off the road," said Clarissa, surprising herself that she was taking control of the situation. Richard and Kevin began to drag the men into the brush. Clarissa looked down the street; there was no way these men had walked here. She started heading further down the road with Maddie close behind, ignoring Richard's calls asking her where she was going. "They must have horses somewhere." She told Maddie in a soft whisper, as if they could be overheard. It was hard to see in the dark, but after several minutes of looking around, they heard the whinnying of a beast, and following the direction, they came across the three horses tied to stakes that had been put into the ground. "What do you plan to do with them? Maddie asked

"These are worth a tidy penny, and we could probably hock them in Regor," she replied as she pulled out the stake, untied the beasts, and led them back to the two men who were now approaching. She handed one off to Kevin, and they led the three horses back to their camp.

"So, what do we do now?" Kevin said desperately after Clarissa had explained the situation.

"We carry on to Regor and meet with this Blake." Clarissa shrugged.

"You still trust them, my lady?" Richard said incredulously and almost patronizingly.

"Oh, I'd never trusted them, Richard. I've never trusted them one bit to be anything other than what they are. However, if my service is of such great value to them, we now hold all the cards. Correct me if I'm wrong, but they were just seeing this as business and not personal."

"She's right there." Maddie agreed. "To go to this much trouble, the Tallymen is playing for big stakes. They will see this as just business by their standards."

"These are dangerous games you play, milady," said Richard sharply. "Heed my counsel. We should just abandon these goods and steer clear of the Tallymen."

"And to do what Richard?" Clarissa said impatiently. "Live as vagabonds? One thing Lincoln was right about is that I may want a life away from the House of Maine, but I still want a comfortable life. We may be able to turn this to our advantage."

"Or it may simply get us killed." Richard snapped back.

Clarissa looked up as she heard the chirping of a bird nearby. "It's dawn, and we still are more than a day away from Regor. We've got time to worry about this, and it's nearly done. Let's just get back on the road."

In silence, the companions packed up the camp and led the wagons back onto the road. Clarissa tied two of the horses to the rear of one of the wagons, but she climbed up on the third. "I'm going to ride ahead, but not far. I'll remain in sight, but at least I'll see something coming before it sees us."

"Or you could get shot off your horse before you see them," stated Richard.

"All you *ever* do is complain. Richard. It is becoming most tiresome. If you don't have anything positive to contribute, please just shut up." Not waiting for an answer, she rode her horse ahead, enjoying the solitude from her companions.

It was late afternoon the following day when the occupants of the two carts finally could see the tops of the spires of Regor. The city was larger than Jilrir and had once been the capitol, and was similar to Clarissa's hometown in many ways. Yet in many aspects, the city was different. The city wall was almost twice as high, and watchtowers pierced the sky, built in a time before the unification of the land when cities maintained their own states.

As Clarissa rode her horse up over a rise, she stared up to see the spires on top of each of these towers, but was yet unable to see the men that stood beneath them looking out for signs of threat. It wasn't needed for there had not been a war in the land since the Maines first came to power two hundred years previously. There were certainly provincial conflicts from time to time, but Regor was so deeply entrenched in Ithia that the conflicts never reached this city. Clarissa stared in wonder. She had never seen anything beyond the grandeur of Jilrir. She stopped her horse, allowing Kevin, who pulled the cart up beside her.

"Is there a problem, milady?" He asked.

"Regor," she said softly.

"What about it?"

"Have you ever seen anything as large as this?" She responded with wonder in her voice.

"I can't say I have, but I'm still not sure what's impressing you."

"There must be fifty thousand people in this city. We could get lost here and never be found."

"You're thinking of staying in Regor?" Kevin frowned.

Clarissa shrugged. "Possibly." She turned to look over her shoulder at the young man. "Would that be such a bad idea?"

It was Kevin's turn to shrug. "No idea. It's not like I'm used to this running and hiding."

Clarissa chuckled. "Regretting coming?"

Kevin pondered this a moment. "It's a bit of this and a bit of that. I don't know. It's great being with you, but part of me is fearful of what the future holds. But I guess once we get some idea of what we're doing, that will probably go."

Clarissa looked back towards the city. "I couldn't have said it better myself. Kevin. Come on, let's go see what the future holds."

She gently whipped up the horse to move forward, and they started heading down the hill towards Regor.

# Chapter Fourteen

## Regor

That was the statutory city guard of the gate, checking people in and out. Had this been morning, there would've been more people around, and it would've taken some time; however, by this time in the afternoon, things were quiet, which wasn't good because the guard generally spent more time fulfilling their duties. A burly-looking man in the great colors of the city guard stepped out of a small hut built beside the gate, which was open, and raised a hand for her to. "Hail and well met, madam," he said in a friendly and cheerful manner. "Please state the nature of your visit to the great city of Regor."

Clarissa was surprised that she was not asked to dismount and looked down at him as she replied. "Delivery of goods."

"How do you intend to stay within the city?"

"I'm not too sure. My business will be conducted quickly, but this is my first visit to Regor, and I would also like to take in some of the sights. Do you have any good playhouses?"

The guard beamed up at her with pride. "Oh, we have the finest playhouses in all of The Land. You should check out the amphitheatre on Orchard Street."

"I will be sure to." Clarissa smiled.

The guard glanced at the two carts coming up behind her. "Are both of these with you?"

"They are indeed." At that moment, the guard began looking down at the vehicles. Clarissa glanced over her shoulder nervously, wondering if there was going to be an issue with her cargo.

"Would you be kind enough to untie your covering?" he said to Richard, who looked uneasy as he jumped down. The experienced guard noticed this, and he too started to look uneasy.

There was nothing they could do if they attacked this man; they would be dead in seconds from archers overhead, standing up on the walls, and she felt sure there would be more guards within the little hut.

All the same, Clarissa's hand went down to rest upon the puffer in her belt. Richard slowly unfastened one of the straps holding down the top and pulled it back. The guard stared wide-eyed, but then a slow smile started across his face, and Clarissa wondered what that meant. He nodded to Richard. "You can strap it back down," he said, then turned around and looked back up at Clarissa. "A cargo like that needs a special permit," he said with a sly smile. "It will cost you five sivs."

"We were already taxed back in Hayburn," Clarissa replied with a frown.

"Oh, I don't think you understand the situation, ma'am." The guard's smile disappeared.

"Pay him, Clarissa," Maddie called from her cart.

With her friend's voice being so urgent, she didn't question it and reached down into her purse to pull out five sivs, a week's pay for someone in the guard's job. She dropped it into his grubby hand, and the money disappeared into his pocket.

He smiled. "Go ahead."

"I thought I was supposed to get a permit?" she asked

"She's new at this game, isn't she?" he said, addressing his question to Maddie.

"Keep going, Clarissa," was all Maddie replied, but she smiled and shrugged at the guard, who shuffled as he headed back to the hut. Confused, Clarissa rode the horse through the gates with the carts following on behind, but she didn't get far into the road before she looked back at Maddie. "What was that about?"

"He took a bribe. It wasn't about a permit."

Clarissa flushed slightly and looked ahead, embarrassed by her own ignorance. "I clearly have a lot to learn in this world of skullduggery."

***

The architecture, although much larger and grander than Jilrir's, was very much the same style, with one major exception: instead of straight roads running north-south, east-west, the roads are winding and twisty. She stopped a couple of times to ask for directions to the Blue Boar Tavern. Despite taking a wrong turn now and then, they eventually saw it. A tall three-story structure with the obvious sign of a blue boar swinging from the second level, she turned down a small driveway that could barely fit the carts. Aware that deliveries were made around the back of most establishments. A short little man came out of the back door. His dress was that of someone from a lower class trying to appear more than he was. The once smart suit, of mediocre quality linen, had seen better days and was threadbare in parts, but his bearing suggested he was a man of substance. "Can I help you?" his tone was considered rough, that of a working man.

"I'm here to see a man called Blake," Clarissa said as she dismounted.

"Aye, well that be me."

"We have a delivery for you."

"Are you from the brewery? 'Cause I expect no deliveries till two days from now."

"No, we're not from the brewery. Do you want this delivery or not?" Clarissa tried to rein in her impatience.

Blake shrugged. "I ain't expecting no deliveries."

"Well, that's considerably frustrating because Mr. Lincoln asked us to deal with this here." Clarissa sniped.

His expression changed, but it was not for the better, as his eyes narrowed. "You're not the usual delivery person for Mr. Lincoln."

"Maybe so, but we are here to make a delivery all the same. My understanding was that he sent someone ahead to inform you."

Even as she said it, it occurred to her that the people who would inform him they were coming would have been those who had tried to steal the goods from them. They would still have made the delivery, but they would have instructed Blake to tell the bogus story that Clarissa had lost the goods.

"Look, Mr. Blake, we have had a long journey, and we're tired." Clarissa jumped down. "I'm not gonna play games with you. We delivered the goods, and we want our payment."

"Wait here." He disappeared back inside, and Clarissa turned to look at her companions, who appeared to be as concerned as she was. She tensed as Blake retired with three other men, but relaxed as he said. "Pull the carts up over there by the storeroom."

The company complied, and leading the carts, they stood watching as the two men started to unload them. Blake counted the goods and checked them off on an inventory sheet. Nothing was said during this time, and Clarissa looked about, realising that should this transaction turn nasty, the only way out was the way they had come in, unless they went through the bar itself. It was not like the Tallymen had filled her with trust, considering what had happened on the road. About half an hour later, the carts were empty. Will you give me anything for these two horses?" she said, referring to the plunder from her encounter stop.

Blake stepped over to them and gave me a quick examination. "I'll give you fifteen for this one, but only ten for this one, which is a lot older." Not being aware of the value of horses, Clarissa simply nodded. "You're two puffers and two carbines short on the manifest. Got an explanation?

"Personally purchased. Please deduct the cost from our fee."

"Well, that pretty much covers the cost of the horses, so let's just say a fair exchange?"

Since Clarissa never paid for the horses in the first place, and ironically, they were probably already owned by the Tallymen, she didn't really have a problem with that.

"Sign here." He handed her the inventory parchment. She automatically signed it, just as she would any official document, with simply the one word 'Clarissa.'

"Now, about our payment?" She said firmly.

Blake looked to one of his men and pointed his thumb towards the back door. The man nodded and went inside. Richard tensed uneasily, wondering what was going on.

"Do you need a place to stay the night before you head back to Hayburn?" Blake asked. "The room is complimentary."

"No, thank you," Clarissa replied, feeling it unwise to stay on the premises of the Tallymen. "But your offer is most appreciated. Now, Mr. Lincoln told me I would have the opportunity to meet with The Master. Can that be arranged?"

Concern across Blake's face. "Do you have any proof that Link told you that?"

"No, I do not."

"Then, unfortunately, ma'am, I cannot introduce you to The Master." Blake shrugged. "No offense, but I don't know who you are, and you're not the typical people I deal with from Hayburn."

"Oh, that's most disappointing, but I understand. Please let The Master know that Clarissa would like to have a word with him, and when we come back for the carts tomorrow, you let me know if he's willing?"

"Sure thing," Blake said as the man he sent inside now came out carrying a metal box. Blake pulled out a small key from his pocket, and as his companion held it, he unlocked it and lifted the lid. A mass of gold coins shone in the afternoon sun. Blake started to count out the money, placing it in Clarissa's cupped hands. Four hundred Sivs was a lot of money, although Clarissa had no idea of its value. Things were bought for her, and she had neither concerned herself with the cost nor the actual financial transactions made by the servants or retainers.

"That's our business concluded," Blake stated. "We will stable your horses for the night and prepare them for your return to Hayburn on the morrow."

Clarissa smiled warmly and shook his hand. "Thank you, Mr Blake. It's an absolute delight doing business with you."

She turned and walked through her companions, who fell in step behind her as she passed each one. Back out on the street, Kevin turned to her with some confusion. "You're not really thinking of going back to Hayburn, are you?"

"No, but I want him to have the opportunity to speak to this The Master, and I didn't have any other excuse to come back." She tied her purse back onto her belt, and it hung heavily, so she pulled her cloak around it. Even she knew that a heavy purse was a draw for a cutpurse. "We need to find somewhere to stay for the night. Does anyone have any recommendations?

No one did, so they wandered down the streets looking about at various Inns as they passed. They found themselves entering the merchants' quarter, where the quality of accommodation drastically improved. One rather upmarket-looking place drew Clarissa's attention. The White Hart was a regal-looking place, and despite the uncomfortable looks of Maddie and Kevin, she ventured inside. She was greeted by a large-chested, round woman who was getting on in age, and she beamed at them until her eyes alighted upon Maddie and Kevin, and the quality of their dress.

"Do you have rooms available for all of us?" Clarissa asked

"We are rather an exclusive establishment." The woman looked down her nose at her companions. "Are you sure you wish to stay here?"

"Are you questioning our ability to pay, or are you just being offensive, Madam?" Clarissa asked tersely.

Noticing the upper-class way Clarissa spoke, her attitude quickly changed. "Oh, my apologies. That was most inappropriate of me. Yes, we do indeed have rooms for all of you. There are fourteen sivs a night."

"Marran's girdle!" Kevin said in shock, not helping with the woman's distrust issues.

"That does, of course, come with dinner and breakfast," the woman advised

"Thank you. We will take them." Clarissa replied.

"We do require payment in advance." The woman said, her eyes surveying Kevin.

Clarissa knew only too well that establishments of this caliber did not require payment in advance, only on departure, and this was another slight to the company. However, she agreed and counted out the coinage on the counter. The woman took it, dropping it into a little slot beside her table, where the coins jingled down to the bottom of the box, which was clearly locked and bolted shut. She then called a young maid, who led them up to their rooms.

Clarissa's room was quite luxurious, with a four-poster bed, although not quite of the caliber of her bedroom back in Jilrir. She pulled off her weapons belt after laying the two puffers on the bedside cabinet, but she didn't get undressed; she simply removed her boots and lay back on the bed. The stench of her feet filled the room, for she had not removed those boots since her last night on the boat. She desperately wanted a bath, so she pulled the bell cord and within a couple of minutes the young maid reappeared. "Any chance I could bathe?" she asked.

"I'll see to it once, milady." The maid curtsied and departed. Clarissa was a tad concerned about the way the maid had addressed her until she realized that was probably how she addressed all clientele within the establishment.

About an hour later, she was lying back in a nice, hot bath, which started to discolor the water as she washed the dirt of the last few days from her body. Once more, she found herself thinking about the future and wondering what to do if she didn't get the meeting with The Master.

Returning to her room, she pondered going to visit Kevin Kurdow in his room, but she was now nice and clean, so why spoil it? Of course, it was ruined by the fact that she had to put on the same clothes she had been wearing, which still smelled of sweat. She made a point of rising early to go into the market and purchase new garments. She woke up at dawn with the sunlight coming down through the window because she hadn't closed the curtains. Having slept in her clothes, it didn't take her long to put her belt back on and stick her two firearms back into that place.

She decided to head out before the others awoke, but as she went down to the lobby, she saw Richard was already there, smoking his pipe. "Good morning, my lady. You're up early."

"I could say the same of you, Richard. I'm going into town to see if I can buy something else to wear that doesn't quite smell like I died in it."

"Do you wish me to accompany you?" It was more of an expectation than an actual question.

"If you wish. I will enjoy your company," she said, giving him a polite reply, for she didn't really care either way.

Richard looked towards the kitchen, where the smell of bacon and eggs was emanating, and sighed. He tapped his pipe on the back of his heel and stood up to join her.

It was quiet in the streets of Regor as they stepped out of their accommodation, and the only sounds that could be heard were the shouts of the traders as they started setting up their stalls in the nearby Market Square. This was the direction they headed in. "I think I agree with you that we should head west." Richard broke the silence.

"Well, aren't you being rather crafty?" Clarissa chuckled, glancing up at him with a side eye.

"I don't know what you mean, my lady."

"You know I'm now thinking of staying here in Regor and not heading west as I originally suggested, but you don't agree with that decision, so you are opening the conversation in the hope that I would bring that up."

"I must admit that was my intention. Since we left Hayburn, we have been heading back toward Jilrir. Indeed, we are now the closest town to the capitol. Your father will be searching for you here if not now, then eventually."

"And you think he'll find us amongst the thousands of people that reside in this city?"

"If I may be so forward, my lady, you do stand out."

"Oh, and how so?" Clarissa replied, amused.

"Your poise. The way you walk. The way you talk. You try to hide it, but you forget. You are clearly of a social class that doesn't fit with your new lifestyle, and that will draw attention as news gets around that the House of Maine is seeking you. It won't take many to put two and two together."

"I'll try to do better, guv," Clarissa smirked, replying in a very poor imitation of the way Kevin Kurdow spoke.

They stepped out into the marketplace, which very much reminded Clarissa of the one at home, with the exception that it was much larger and the fair on offer was of a more suitable quality for her station, or rather, her former station. She had to visit several different traders to purchase a new outfit, each specializing in a different type of garment, such as trousers, shirts, and jackets. As she stopped at the milliner's, she noticed a hood that matched other goods she had purchased. It had a large brow, and she considered that this would better conceal her features than the hat she wore. She purchased it and placed it with her other goods. Obviously, being both a gentleman and a man of service, Richard carried her shopping.

"I've been meaning to ask you something, Richard," Clarissa said as they headed back to the inn.

"Well, that sounds ominous, my lady."

"No, no, it's nothing serious, I was just curious about why you made the decision to help me back in Jilrir."

"Well, it was mostly impulsive, but I suppose even an impulsive act has a reason behind it. In fact, there are a couple of reasons. First of all, I was tired of serving the most odious man I have ever known, and as a retainer to the royal family, I would never be permitted to resign my post." He stopped and sighed. "But if you want the honest truth, a beauty such as yours can turn any man's head."

Clarissa flushed lightly. "You killed a man and left your position because you fancy me?"

Richard chuckled. "When you put it as simply as that, it sounds positively terrible. You were, however, in a state of distress, and it was the honourable act to take."

She raised an eyebrow at him. "You see me as some sort of damsel in distress from some fairy tale?"

Richard sighed and shook his head with another chuckle. "You have a considerable talent to trivialize anything I say, my lady."

"Oh, to be honest, I find it quite romantic that you want to be my knight in shining armor even though it was me who came to your rescue."

"Touché, my lady. You have proved incredibly versatile, but you will need to use your wits to the full if you are to come out of this unscathed. However, it is your companions who are taking the greater risk."

"Oh, and just how so?"

"As I believe it's already been stated, you may receive some punishment for your humiliation of the king and fleeing the House of Maine, but the rest of us will be hanged as fast as it takes to sign the execution order."

"Oh, I don't think that's so. You will at least receive a trial." Clarissa surmised.

"Maybe I will due to my former social standard, but Maddie and Kurdow, and possibly even Taylor, will not, although on the latter, she may do so as not to offend the Church of Ilya."

"Nobody is with me against their will, and they're welcome to leave at any time," Clarissa said tensely, trying to offset the feeling of guilt she had that she was responsible for their lives.

"It may be a good idea if you force that issue. Kurdow and Maddie are not particularly great value in your desire to evade the House of Maine."

"Oh, I completely disagree with you there, Richard. Maddie has streetwise skills I don't possess, and I imagine you don't either. As we walk into the underbelly of society, her insights are most valuable. As for Kevin, I trust him more than anyone."

Richard looked a little offended by this, but he did not comment on it other than to say, "Maybe before he knew your true identity, but that relationship was based on a lie, and I heard his comments to you that first day we left Jilrir. He is certainly not comfortable with your new position."

"We must agree to disagree on that one also," Clarissa responded as they stopped outside the inn. "As you said yourself, a pretty face can turn the head of any man, and Kevin's feelings for me may be stronger than you think. Of all the people in our company, I doubt he will leave my side unless I compel him to."

Without letting Richard respond to that or elaborating on her reasoning, she pulled open the door of the inn and stepped back inside. Rather than return to their rooms, they made straight for the dining hall, both quite hungry and eager for the bacon and eggs that permeated the ground floor. Maddie and Kevin were already there, and halfway through their meal, Richard and Clarissa joined them. "Is Taylor still asleep?"

"No, Milady," Kevin said with a mouthful of bacon. "She has gone into town to visit the temple of Illya.

Clarissa tensed. "Was that wise to let her? Who knows what she was going to say?

"With all due respect, milady," said Kevin defensively. "I do not believe I was under any sort of instructions to stop her from going wherever she will."

"I don't have a good feeling about this." Clarissa sighed.

# Chapter Fifteen

## *Temples and Taverns*

The temple of Illya near the center of Regor was vast in comparison to the little place in Heron Bay. It towered over the surrounding buildings and featured a quite Gothic design. It had not been built as a temple—at least not one dedicated to Illya—and had been repurposed for this purpose many years before. Taylor was not quite sure how long it had been in the hands of her church, but it had been so for as long as anyone alive today could remember. As she walked up the twenty or thirty marble steps outside, she wasn't sure what she was going to do or say. Her departure from Heron Bay had been without the consent of her mistress, and although she could argue that she had no choice, she was not entirely sure if she wanted Clarissa Maine to be declared an enemy of the church. Such an act was effectively a death sentence and would have repercussions with the House of Maine; yet, she could not lie.

Two men stood at the doorway in the livery of the Third Order. Soldiers who had taken holy vows to defend the church and its interests blocked her entrance. She was not wearing her clerical robes, so she slipped out the small silver medallion from under her shirt, revealing the mark of a priestess. They spoke no words, but as soon as their eyes alighted upon it, they stepped aside, allowing her entry, and then she thanked them as she passed into the grand hallway. She gasped as she looked at the splendor of the room, which rose two stories. It was lit by leaded windows, showing scenes from the holy work, the Book of Illya. Large granite pillars painted white rose to a skylight that covered the ceiling, colored in amber to give the room a sunlit feel.

"Welcome." A young woman approached her, dressed in the white robes of a Feffer, an acolyte in training for ordination. "Are you one with the Goddess of Justice?"

Taylor smiled at her. "I am indeed, sister. I am Taylor Hetherington of the Second Order."

The Feffer gave a slight bow as she became aware of the stranger's superiority. "It is an honor to meet you, Sister Taylor. Are you joining us at the Regor branch of the church?

"Alas, no. I am posted at Heron Bay, but I seek counsel with the high priestess."

"Of course, come with me," the young girl said, leading her down to a set of great doors at the end of the hall. Two more of the armed men swung the grand doors open, and they entered a more modest area of the temple where the walls of the corridors were made of simple marble. He passed all the priestesses and temple staff who merely nodded politely as the Feffer led her to the office of the highest-ranking priestess in the city.

Sister Mary Acker was a little older than Taylor and apparently quite young for her position. As she paid Taylor and the Feffer to come in at the latter's knock, she looked up with curiosity from behind a large oak desk in the center of the circular office.

A slight smile crossed her face as a look of recognition lit up in her eyes. "Taylor, what a pleasant surprise. It must be at least five years since I last saw you. Come in, come in." The high priestess rose from her seat, and Taylor relaxed as she recognized the woman who now came around to hug her.

"You are a high priestess?" Taylor chuckled, returning the embrace.

"Oh, don't sound so surprised." Mary returned with a tone of mock offence. "A lot has happened since our days as Feffers in Malint."

"I'm sure it has, but the idea that you made it high priestess before I did is frankly beyond belief," Taylor said jokingly. "I guess I should congratulate you."

Mary chuckled. "Come sit down. Tina, would you see to it that some tea is brought to us?"

Tina nodded and stepped out of the room, closing the door behind her. "So what brings you to Regor. I can assume by your surprise at seeing me, it was not a visit to engage in some nostalgia."

The smile disappeared from Taylor's face. Her friend looked back at her with some concern as she saw it. "I seem to have got myself into a bit of trouble. I'm not looking for help, but I am seeking guidance and possibly even instruction."

Mary smiled softly and patted her friend's arm reassuringly. "I'm sure it's nothing that cannot be resolved. Tell me your story."

"A few days ago, a young woman came to the temple in Heron Bay. The officers of the House of Maine were pursuing her. I was assigned to escort her around the town while she sorted herself out, but the pursuit of her came quickly, and she fled by boat, and I had no option but to join her."

Mary's eyes widened, and a look of surprise crossed her fair features. "Please tell me you are not talking about Lady Clarissa Maine?" she said with considerable concern.

It was Taylor's time to look surprised. "You know of this matter already?"

"As the high priestess representing the church in Regor, I am automatically an honorary member of the City Council. The mayor's office sent word that the House of Maine is in pursuit of Lady Clarissa, and we are to inform them should she seek sanctuary within these walls."

"I do not believe that would be justice," Taylor replied, concerned now and regretting that she had come here.

"All I know is that they pursue this girl; I do not know why. I cannot judge your statement until I do." Mary frowned.

The pair fell silent as Tina entered the room, carrying a tray with a silver teapot and two cups. He placed it on the desk, bowed to the high priestess, and then to Taylor before departing. As the door was shut, they continued.

"Clarissa was betrothed to the Crown Prince, and she did not wish the union," Taylor advised. "As such, she fled the household of the Baron."

"And she is here with you in Regor?" Mary sounded surprised.

"She is, but she's not seeking sanctuary here." Taylor's voice was earnest and almost imploring, urging Mary not to reveal this to the city officials.

Mary stood up and began pouring the tea, her face furrowed and her expression heavy as she considered the situation. "This is truly an affair of state, but we should not become embroiled in it."

"Are we not automatically embroiled in this situation when an injustice is clearly taking place?" Taylor tilted her head questioningly.

"How so?"

"The girl is being forced to marry a man against her will," Taylor said determinedly. "Surely that's an injustice."

"That depends on your perspective. Arranged marriages are the norm for the ruling classes of the land and have been so since there was such a thing as a ruling class." Mary sighed.

"The perpetuation of an injustice does not make it just," Taylor said firmly.

Mary sighed again. She handed the cup to her friend and sat back down behind her desk. "This, my dear friend, goes way beyond my pay grade and is a matter for the Esselar," she said, referring to the overall head of the church.

"I'm quite sure it does, but the Esselar is far away in Aranar, and I cannot wait for her counsel."

Mary's brow furrowed as she pondered the situation, her face a mixture of concern and indecision. "What would you have me say? She asked eventually.

"I wish to see how this plays out. I want to remain a companion to Clarissa Maine for as long as she will have me and for as long as the church permits. I don't know which path she is taking, but the political ramifications of these actions are not insignificant. However, I believe it will be beneficial for the church to find out. So what do you say, do I have you're leave to continue?"

Mary sipped her tea, looking at Taylor over the rim of her cup. She pondered the request as she placed the cup back upon the saucer. "I leave you to be the judge of your own actions, Taylor. I pass no judgment on this, but nor do I impede you."

Taylor clearly understood the implications of what the high priestess had just told her. She was permitted to continue without being explicitly given permission. Essentially, she was negating any responsibility for any potential negative outcomes for the church resulting from Taylor's choices.

"I understand, and I take this on my own shoulders. I will remain in the company of Clarissa Maine and see what comes."

***

It was mid-morning by the time Clarissa Maine returned to the Blue Boar. She did not take the entire company and she had only Richard at her side. The others were told that if she did not report back within two hours, they would be in some sort of trouble.

The tavern was closed when they arrived, but Blake answered the door upon knocking. He seemed to be in a much more pleasant mood as he let them in. The Blue Boar was only a slight improvement on the fatted calf back in Jilrir, with a straw-covered floor that stank and needed refreshing.

"Did you get an opportunity to speak to The Master?" Clarissa came straight to the point.

"Indeed, I did, and he has come down here to meet with you," Blake replied, leading them through to his backroom and a dingy little office that appeared to be in somewhat of a disarray, indicating the disorganized temperament of Blake. The Master was seated behind the desk, as if he owned the place, and he probably did. He was a large, bull-shouldered man, impeccably dressed, indicating a man of financial means. However, it was not in the style of someone born to wealth; it was garish and over-the-top, with bright colours that indicated wealth but not taste. When he spoke, this only validated Clarissa's initial observation.

He had a beaming, jovial smile as he stood up from behind his desk and stepped around to greet her with a slight bow. "Lady Clarissa, may I tell you this is an absolute delight to meet you?"

"Likewise, Master," Clarissa responded out of politeness rather than genuine feeling. "Do you have a name, sir?"

"I am simply known as the Master, and I must say, I'm intrigued by the message for Mr. Lincoln of your interest in being part of our operations. I had to ensure that it wasn't All Fools' Day."

"Well, I can certainly understand that, Sir." Clarissa smiled. "But these are not normal circumstances."

"Indeed, and I would certainly like to know what circumstances those are."

"Oh, I think the only thing you need to know is that my association with the House of Maine under my family is no longer a consideration in what I do and what I hope to achieve. My personal affairs are not part of this business."

The Master pondered this but said, "Understood, Lady Clarissa. Come take a seat."

Clarissa sat in a modest chair and crossed her legs as the Master returned to his seat behind the desk.

"What exactly do you hope to do for us, my lady?" The Master leaned his elbows upon the desk and templed his fingers.

"Oh, let's not play games, Master." Clarissa rolled her eyes. "Mr. Lincoln was so eager for me to join you, he tried to set us up on the road by stealing your own cargo. Therefore, I imagine that I am holding at least three of the four aces right now."

The Master chuckled. "Yes, and you handled that situation quite well, although the loss of three of our men is quite a shame."

"Well, you can let that be a lesson to you, but I'm not to be trifled with. I placed no value on the lives of men who want to cross me." It wasn't true ... at least it wasn't on the day she sat in the Master's office.

"Understood. However, to become part of the Tallymen, you need to pass your initiation. Merely a matter of routine, but one this convention does not permit me to circumnavigate."

"Is this yet more of your games, The Master?"

"No, no, not at all, Lady Clarissa, merely a time-honoured tradition that I am not willing to dispense with even for The Second Lady of Jilrir."

"I hope you are not thinking of me as one of your typical street thugs, The Master. If I were to join you, I would expect a position of authority from the ground up."

"That is certainly quite an ask, but I can see my way to giving you the position of a sector Lieutenant." The Master shrugged.

Clarissa scoffed, "That is merely a little more than a thug in a nice suit. No, I passed your little test back on the road when you tried to steal our carts. I have proven my resourcefulness and ability. I do not intend to participate in your initiation and expect a position in keeping with my social standing."

The Master sighed. "Then I think we have nothing more to talk about, for I cannot agree to such terms."

"That is your loss, Master." Clarissa started to rise from her chair, closely followed by Richard. "Thank you for this audience, and I will bid you good day."

The Master rose from his chair, and Clarissa had the sinking feeling that he was about to call her bluff. He said nothing, but his eyes looked over her as if considering something, and as she turned towards the door, he stopped her. "Do you still have any influence as a member of the House of Maine?"

Clarissa turned back, tilting her head slightly. "I still bear the name, but that's about all."

"That may be good enough; it is a name that instils fear and influence. Please come back and sit down."

Clarissa deliberately hesitated, then complied. "Do not waste my time, Master."

"I will make you a city captain on the condition we can use your name as leverage or with the authorities."

"In all honesty," Clarissa responded. "My name cannot speak on behalf of my family or the House of Maine and will only bring the wrath of my father."

"The people we deal with will not know that. Your father is a ruthless bastard, and he is not known for his consideration for those of a lesser class." The Master smiled.

Clarissa chuckled. "Oh, I think my father is a ruthless bastard enough to strip me of my titles under any authority I may have once had."

"No, I don't think so." The Master mused. My operatives in Jilrir tell me your flight is a matter of incredible embarrassment for him. While he may be pursuing you, he is not about to advertise a rift with his only daughter. The word on the street is that you left against your will and not that you are at odds with him."

"There is a glaring hole in your plan. I cannot exactly exercise the authority of the House of Maine for the moment I reveal myself, my father would have me taken into custody."

"I will make sure your appearances anywhere are well-controlled and that we have all the avenues covered. I personally guarantee your safety. Well, at least from the House of Maine. The Tallymen has many enemies, and they are not all from the state. You will deal with the more influential people that we want to do business with, but are not as interested in doing business with us, let's say, lesser mortals."

"I'm not totally convinced that your power extends to guarantee my safety." Clarissa frowned. "How could this be the case when the House of Maine has absolute authority over everything?"

The Master chuckled. "Oh, I assure you that most city officials are on our payroll. Their loyalty is to coin not your father, and those who do not so do so willingly respond instead to imaginative threats. The Tallymen can guarantee your safety with almost ninety percent certainty."

"And what if I meet the ten percent?" Clarissa chuckled.

"Lady Clarissa, you have to understand that the Tallymen is not a royal ball. There is inherent danger to our work, and we're all targets. If you want absolute safety, I suggest you return to your father's house and live your life there."

"Understood, Master." Clarissa rose and extended her hand. "I accept your generous offer. I look forward to doing business with you.

"Excellent." The Master positively beamed at her.

"Give me a day to find a more permanent residence for my team, for indeed I am bringing them along with me and shall return on the morrow to further discuss my responsibilities. How does that sound to you?"

"Positively delightful, Lady Clarissa, I will see you then."

***

"Well, if we're going to stay in Regor, we're going to have to find a place to live," said Maddie when, about an hour later, Clarissa was sitting with the others in the bar, enjoying a fine lunch.

"What about we just stay here in the inn?" suggested Kevin.

"Long-term residence generally draws interesting questions," replied Maddie.

"And no doubt Trent will search for me in inns and taverns," Clarissa said as she stabbed her potato.

"Also, we cannot control the security of the premises, and since we appear to be going down a path of nefarious activity, we cannot take risks," said Richard.

"Time to find our new home," Clarissa said and stuffed the potato in her mouth.

# Chapter Sixteen

# Two Two Three Sycamore Street

Property was not exactly cheap in the affluent city of Regor. However, the companions managed to obtain a reasonably priced townhouse just off the merchants' quarter, one of those that was not particularly wide but went up three stories, at two two three Sycamore Street.

It was leased for three months in Maddie's name, as the person least likely to be on the authorities' radar. Although Clarissa still did most of the talking since Maddie's working-class Jilrian accent didn't quite fit the upper-middle-class residents, it would have raised concerns.

Two Two Three Sycamore Street lay in the fairly upmarket region of Regor. It was beyond the purse of many residents; however, Clarissa Maine required premises where all her companions could remain together. There were only three bedrooms, divided among the company. Clarissa and Maddie shared one, Richard and Kevin shared another, and Taylor had a room to herself. The young priestess hadn't said anything about her meeting with the head of the Regor branch of her church, but Clarissa couldn't help but notice that she had become much more relaxed. The truth was that the tacit approval for her to remain with Clarissa assuaged much of the guilt she felt for involving herself with the companions who were clearly stepping well outside of the law. She had no idea how long they could reside within that city, but inns and boarding houses would be the first obvious place to search for them. Clarissa had hoped that renting a fairly affluent residence would be the last place they would consider looking. Of course, pursuing a more lavish lifestyle meant they would require a fairly substantial income.

"I suppose I could go back on the game, but I'm not as young as I once was," Maddie said with much reluctance as they discussed the issue over breakfast one morning. "However, I am getting much older, and my street value has considerably declined."

"Whilst I can hardly argue that my life these days is particularly virtuous," Clarissa smirked. "I seriously don't want to live off the earnings of prostitution from one of my friends."

"Is it just the friends aspect you have a problem with?" Maddie chuckled. "Like you don't have a particular problem living off the earnings of such an activity in general?"

Clarissa pondered this for a moment before looking over at Taylor. "Where does your church lie in this regard?"

Taylor laid down her fork, took a sip of her tea, mulling over the idea of organized prostitution. "Liberty is one of the cornerstones of the faith. Illya is the Goddess of Justice, not law. As long as the transaction is between two consenting adults, she has no problem with it. However, a third party profiting from the transaction is a more grey area because it is constantly subject to abuse. Whilst it is not morally wrong to employ someone to provide such services, it all depends on the nature of the employment."

"What do you mean, not morally wrong?" Richard said haughtily. "Surely, for a woman of Lady Clarissa's standing, it would be unethical to engage in such activity."

Taylor actually let out a chuckle. "Are you seriously telling me that prostitution is a greater crime than murder, theft, and piracy? Come now, Richard, are you so virtuous that you're going to argue that one should only lie with another within wedlock?"

"Someone such as Lady Clarissa, I most certainly argue that point," he said, growing defensive of the Second Lady. "Her virtue is of the highest value."

Clarissa choked on her tea, put the cup down, and stared uncomfortably out of the window.

"I see," Taylor replied with a little whimsy in her voice. "You, Sir, are of the same social standing as Lady Clarissa. Are you going to honestly put your hand on your heart here and tell me that you're untouched by a woman?"

Richard flushed slightly and glanced down at his plate. "Well, no, but it is different in my case."

"Oh, really, and how so?" Taylor responded, although she already knew the answer.

Richard steeled himself, raised his eyes, and fixed his gaze upon the young priestess. "I am a man, Sister Taylor. "

"Ah, I see," Taylor smiled softly. "I assume that because a woman can get pregnant, she has to guard her virtue more fastidiously. Is that what you're saying?"

"Of course." Richard acted like it was obvious.

"And you have no role in bringing forth new life within a woman?" Taylor tilted her head. "You believe that because you do not bear the child, you have no responsibility for the result of your actions."

"It is the woman who assumes that the risk, Sister Taylor," Richard argued with growing irritation. "If she chooses to spread her legs for a man, then she should take the consequences."

"So you believe that you should only fornicate with a woman that you do not have any respect or concern for. A double standard, if you ask me, and it is not justice." Taylor shrugged dismissively.

"Such a woman does not deserve any respect or consideration and has little value," Richard shouted, banging his fist on the table.

He did not see the slap coming, but he felt it hard across his cheek. Maddie was now standing up at his side, glaring down at him. "So, oh noble bloody lord, the likes of me are worthless in your eyes."

Richard, startled by this act, recovered quickly as he rubbed his face and looked up at her. "Well, I..."

"You know, Richard," said Clarissa quite calmly. "I think you should excuse yourself from the table and go outside before this escalates."

Richard looked at her, then back up at the glaring Maddie, and then at all the eyes around the table that were staring at him. He pushed his chair back and rose to his feet, took a simple bow, and said, "Ladies. Mr. Kurdow. If you will excuse me." He strode from the room.

Maddie resumed her seat. "I'm incredibly sorry about that, Maddie," Clarissa said softly, placing her hand on hers.

"Oh, don't worry about it, darling," she smiled. "It's not like I've not heard his views consistently over the years, I just consider it inappropriate to voice them in my presence."

"But it is not the same," Clarissa responded. "You should not have to hear such things at all, and such an attitude should not be prevalent in our company. Prostitution is not a crime. At least not in the Province of Ithia, and one should not treat someone with disrespect just because of their chosen profession. However, this does give me an idea." A slight smile crossed her face. "Such activities are usually in lower-class establishments, and while I'm not referring to you, Maddie, they are generally less educated women."

"What are you exactly suggesting?" Kevin asked.

Clarissa pondered. "What if we were to have, let's say, more upmarket women working out of this house with more upmarket clients at a higher rate of pay?"

Kevin snorted, "Where on earth are you gonna find upmarket women willing to prostitute themselves even if it's in a fancy whore house?"

"Oh, Kevin, you are so naïve." Maddie chuckled. "There are women of all classes who spread their legs for coin. However, the more upmarket ones generally work by word of mouth and visit clients in their residences or more classy inns. They generally don't work out of premises."

"Could we not achieve such a goal and have this house as a place of entertainment?" Clarissa suggested.

"Well, I'm pretty sure that the Tallymen already has that area business wrapped up exclusively," Maddie said. "You would need permission to start such an establishment in competition with other members."

"And what do you rate my chances of receiving such permission?" Clarissa asked.

"The Tallymen operates on the toughest kid on the block idea. As a newcomer, even if the top dog gives you a high position, respect is still given to the last man standing. Someone with an established profitable business is not going to take you stepping on their territory without a fight."

Again, Clarissa pondered, and another crazy thought popped into her head. A sly, dry smile crossed her lips as she tilted her head and told Maddie, "You know your way around the skin trade. See what you can do to find out who the top dogs in this line of business are."

Maddie frowned slightly, wondering where Clarissa was going with this, but she simply nodded and agreed.

***

Richard Kyle sat on the front step of the house, smoking his pipe and pondering the new life he had stepped into. To say he had regrets would be an understatement. His hasty decision to help Clarissa Maine had literally destroyed his life as he knew it. The path she was now taking was not one he wished to follow. Yet, he had betrayed the Crown Prince, and in doing so, he had betrayed his king. This was a crime from which there was no coming back. He was destined for the gallows if ever caught.

"A sheckle for your thoughts," came the voice of the woman who, by proxy, had become his mistress. He glanced back at Clarissa, who was coming out of the front door, but he said nothing and just stared back out into the street. He did not move nor look back as the young woman came and sat down beside him on the step. "I understand if you want to leave us, Richard," she said softly. "I neither asked you nor expected you to come with us, but come you did. I appreciate your support and value your counsel, but if you are not content with the path I'm taking, I will not protest at your departure."

Richard did not answer immediately; he continued to stare out into the street, looking at nothing in particular, and drew once more on his pipe. Clarissa coughed slightly as he blew out the smoke. He let the words mull over in his head. Every fibre of his being wanted to turn upon her and say he was out, that he would leave, but instead he found himself looking down with his feet and muttering, "And where would I go, my lady?"

Clarissa shrugged. "Wherever you want. That's not for me to say."

"I am a marked man, Lady Clarissa. I cannot return home, nor can I see any of my family again. I have no skills beyond being a prince's man. Since there is only one prince in the entire Land and his father will have me hanged without a second thought, my survival odds are very, very small."

"Oh, come now, Richard." Clarissa smiled. "You have a skilled sword hand. There were many who would pay for you to bear that sword in their name."

Richard snorted. "And how different is becoming a mercenary from the life that I would find in serving you. There are few legitimate positions for a sword for hire, and most of those are as a guard for some slummy warehouse or some caravan crossing the plains. The pay would be pitiful, and the lifestyle would be that of a peasant. I do not consider myself an arrogant man, but I do consider myself a civilised man, and the lifestyle of a pauper does not appeal to me."

It was Clarissa's turn to snort. "Well, I'm certainly not guaranteeing you a life of luxury here, Richard. I have been winging it ever since we stepped outside the walls of Jilrir."

"Oh, you have done all right for yourself. Look at this house, most of this city could not afford to walk down this street, let alone reside in such a property."

"We only have this for as long as my purse holds out; unless we come up with ideas on how to replenish it, it will not last long." Clarissa sighed and stared out into space as she bit her lip and gathered her thoughts into words. "It is not like we live in a system where have-nots can raise themselves to become haves. Maddie may talk about how hard it is to rise within a criminal syndicate like the Tallymen, but it is certainly doable. However, rising in a legitimate business is not possible. The upper social classes have that neatly tied up, most incestuously. Businesses are passed down to sons rather than the best employees. If you were to start your own business, you would be ruthlessly crushed by those currently in power. So, don't fool yourself into thinking that legitimate businesses out there are any more legitimate than what we are suggesting here. As sister Taylor says, legality does not make it right. The law is there to protect the rich, not to help those who aspire to join their ranks."

"That does not make running a brothel right." Richard snapped. "You are the Second Lady of Jilrir. It is unethical for you to take such a role."

"Oh, by Marran's girdle, Richard, when are you going to get it through that thick skull of yours that I have left all that behind? It may not have happened yet, but eventually my father, or even the king, will remove any titles they once held. Hopefully, to save face, they will claim I am dead. And I will finally be free to choose my own life."

"Yet your choices lead to darkness, my lady." Richard sighed. "And I fear for you. You would not have been able to escape Jilrir without my help, and having chosen to do that, I feel responsible for your safety and welfare."

Clarissa gently placed a hand upon his thigh. He looked down at it, then finally turned to face her, looking up at him with the softest smile. "I may not have put it into words, and I may not even be able to do that now, but I do appreciate what you have done for me. For all of us, it's true: we would not have escaped Heron Bay if it were not for you. I value that sword arm greatly, and I value you greatly. I would hate to lose you, but I do not want to hold you here by a sense of duty or guilt. I want you to remain with me because you truly want to."

When later retelling the story, neither of them can explain how it happened. However, the long and the short of it was that Richard leaned in towards her, and she reached up towards him. His arm slipped around her shoulders, and her arm slipped around his waist, and they kissed—gentle and giving from both of them. Clarissa felt a tingle in her stomach, and Richard felt a stirring in his loins as the kiss continued without respite.

"What the fuck?" They broke the kiss suddenly, startled by the sound of the familiar voice.

"Kevin," Clarissa called, her arms withdrawing rapidly from the young Lord. But Kevin did not allow her to continue as he walked back into the house and slammed the door behind him.

# Chapter Seventeen

# The Machinations of Master Sergeant Trent

Master Sergeant Julian Trent had served in the Palace Guard of the House of Maine for almost thirty years as a member of the provincial army as a ranger. He was considered among the elite, and for the past three years, he had served as the second-in-command responsible for protecting the First Family of Ithia. The Baron himself had given him his current orders. Take as many men as he required and pursue his daughter, Lady Clarissa Maine, and bring her back unharmed—all other considerations to be considered irrelevant.

Trent was neither a bad man nor a particularly good one; he followed his orders, whatever they may be, without allowing his personal considerations to get in the way. The mark of what was considered a good officer. He picked out two of his best men, Lucas and Bailey. And after discovering that Richard Kyle had left the city without the prince's leave, he put two and two together, deciding Clarissa was heading for Heron Bay. He set off at once in pursuit, while scouts were sent to other neighboring towns to inform their leadership to be on the lookout for her, just in case.

He had confidently believed his pursuit was over when he encountered Clarissa at the dock in the little fishing town and clearly underestimated her, not believing that she would resist violently. The fact that she shot him was certainly a wake-up call, even though the wound was minor.

However, he was more concerned when his companions started firing back. The Baron Maine was an unforgiving bastard, and returning to report that they had killed his daughter would have seen him on the gallows. So it was when they helped him up; he was not in his best mood, and the intense pain in his shoulder worsened with the movement. Fortunately, being close to the Illyan temple, the lead ball was removed from his shoulder, and his wound was quickly healed.

He did not, however, hang around, considering the type of vessel that Clarissa had departed in; it was unlikely they would go further than Hayburn. The three palace guards set out at once along the long road to that town. He was well aware that it would take him longer to get there than it would for her, for there was no direct road and they would have to travel some way back to Jilrir before they could turn off the road. They could travel across land, but the rugged terrain would have made their progress even slower.

However, by the time they arrived in that town, unbeknownst to him, Clarissa had already started on her journey to Regor. It didn't take him long to find out about the arrival of the Lady Luck and that the Second Lady was wanted for the crime of piracy, although the authorities did not know her name at that time.

"I want the records of this crime to be destroyed," Trent told the mayor when he visited the town hall, invoking the authority of the Baron. "And I don't want this matter pursued."

"Piracy is considered one of the worst crimes one can commit, Master Trent," The aged mayor protested. "And you're asking me to turn a blind eye to it."

"It is a bigger crime to sully the name of the House of Maine Mayor Pottswait. This is not a request. The Baron himself will deal with the Lady Clarissa, and she is not to be treated like a criminal."

"Yet she *is* a criminal, Master Trent," Pottswait growled.

Trent slammed his fist on the mayor's desk, causing him to jump. "She is a Maine, Pottswait. You are here by the leave and appointed by the Baron himself. If you wish to challenge him, I'm sure you can go to Jilrir and discuss the matter with him personally. Until then, I am operating under his authority to take any action that I deem necessary to ensure the safe return of his daughter, and I will eliminate anything that gets in my way."

"Are you threatening me, Master Trent?" Pottswait stood up from behind his desk, fear in his eyes.

"Implicitly, my good sir. Now your responsibility is to find out where she went after she arrived."

The mayor sighed. "I shall do what I can, Master Trent, but this is a free city, and we do not keep tabs on the residents or visitors."

However, luck would be on Trent's side. He and his men stayed in an inn for the next two days, waiting and hoping for news and even patrolling the streets in the hope of randomly running into her. On the third morning, the mayor summoned them, and Trent went over to the town hall once again.

"I have a possible sighting of her, although it cannot be confirmed. Indeed, the sighting of her actually takes the term too far. A man matching the description of this Richard Kyle was arrested for attempted assault on one of our more affluent citizens, and the victim reported that he was with a woman who matches the description you gave of Lady Clarissa."

Trent sighed and smiled. "Well, that is both interesting yet concerning. May I meet with this man?"

The mayor shook his head."Unfortunately, not. On the same day this man was arrested, a jailbreak occurred. A firearm killed the guard on duty, and both he and another prisoner escaped."

"Hmm." Trent pondered and paced in front of the desk before turning back to the old man. "And who was this other prisoner?"

"Charles Lincoln, a known senior member of the Tallymen." The mayor said uneasily.

"And you have no idea where either of these has gone, I suppose," Trent said dispondantly.

"Oh, we're quite sure that Lincoln will be holed up in one of the many establishments the Tallymen owns." The mayor advised. "They have quite a few legitimate businesses throughout the city."

"While I am fairly certain that Lady Clarissa is *not* involved with the Tallymen, we need to put every effort into finding this man. I want your full resources on the job." Trent demanded.

The mayor looked horrified. "Surely you must be aware, Master Trent, the Tallymen has its fingers in every pie, and it is a very influential and powerful organization. Finding Lincoln will not be easy, and a lot of important people will not be happy."

Trent leaned over his desk and growled. "Let me make it easier for you, sir. You will utilize every resource you have; every man, woman, and child in the employ of the estate and mobilized in the hunt. I *will* find Clarissa Maine if it's the last thing I ever do."

"I really don't think you will like the hornet's nest you are opening, Master Sergeant Trent. The Tallymen is not a street gang, even though some of its activities may fall into that category. There are people behind that organization with a mutually beneficial agreement that we do not interfere in their activities."

"What you are saying is you are on the payroll of the Tallymen." Trent's growl deepened.

"Sir, everybody is on the payroll or in some way under the influence of the Tallymen. Cross the line, and you'll make enemies that you do not want to have."

"That sounds like a threat, Mr. Mayor. Do you know what happens to men who challenge agents of the Baron? They are hanged, Pottswait."

"Take it as a warning. You don't want to wake up one morning and find your body floating in the river."

"Sir, you are forgetting one very important thing." Trent stood upright.

"Oh, and what exactly is that?"

"Whatever influence you think members of this Tallymen may have, the biggest bastard on the block is Azrael Maine. Now, there are certain protocols one would normally follow in these circumstances, but we're talking about his daughter. A member of his family and I assure you that anyone, including yourself, who stands in the way of finding her will not just be hanged but will have their heads on a pike outside of this town hall. Are we understood?"

The mayor shifted uncomfortably in his chair before finally letting out a long sigh. "You are understood, Master Trent. Give me a few days, and we will locate this Lincoln.

"You have one day, Mr. Mayor. Twenty-six hours from now, I will be back here, and you will have an answer for me. The longer we wait, the further she gets away."

As it turned out, the mayor did not require the full twenty-six hours, and a message came to the inn where Trent and his men were staying shortly before he was about to retire for the night. Instead, he hurried over to the town hall when an exhausted and distressed-looking mayor had information for him. "The man you seek is staying in the Blue Boar and is owned by the Tallymen as one of their legitimate cover businesses. It is also a known headquarters of the Tallymen, but I wish to warn you one more time, entering those premises without the Tallymen's permission is tantamount to declaring war on them."

"Oh, trust me, Mr. Mayor, if they are harboring Clarissa Maine, the days of the Tallymen are numbered. You will assign me twenty of your best city guards. We will raid the Blue Boar and take this man into custody. However, I will give you all a warning. If this man turns out not to be there, I will assume, rightly or wrongly, that you are complicit in warning him. Are we understood?"

The startled look on the mayor's face told Trent everything he needed to know, for indeed he was about to warn the Tallymen of the Master Sergeant's intentions.

It was still dark when he and his two men met with the small company of city guards. He did not tell them the purpose of the raid; he simply said they were to secure the building. Indeed, he knew he was working with men who may well be on the Tallymen's payroll, but since they were so low down, it was unlikely they knew the location of its headquarters or why the Blue Boar was important.

Trent wasn't naïve enough to believe that the Tallymen would not have these premises unguarded, and sure enough, as he had his men approach from different directions, he made out shadowy figures on the roof and down the alleyways surrounding it. One of these men was a fairly renowned Archer who quickly dispatched the two men on the roof with neat shots with a bow from across the street. The city guard made their way around the buildings, dispatching other lookouts. He knew full well the doors would be secured. So the instruction was given to enter through the windows. The smashing of glass broke the silence of the dawn as a couple of his men entered the main bar before all fell silent. Then, moments later, they opened the front door, but it was clear no one had gotten word of them, for as the city guard swarmed over the premises, they were taken completely by surprise and offered very little resistance.

A couple of rough-looking men were pulled out into the reception area where Trent was waiting. "Tell me where I will find Lincoln?" he said, stepping up to the three men in front of him. Just then, the three men lowered their eyes and stood stoically, saying nothing. Trent sighed and looked at each in turn before quickly pulling out his sword and thrusting it through the belly of one of the men, who screamed in pain as he staggered back, and the sword slid out of him. Fair across the eyes of the others."

"He's at the back in the office," one blurted out in terror.

Without another word, Trent and his two companions turned and headed to the back of the ball. There was a sudden loud explosion as he opened the door to Lincoln's quarters. Wood splintered in the wall beside him, and he stared in horror at the young man ripping the puffer weapon, which now smoked. Lincoln had tried to kill him, a young woman at his side screamed. Trent nearly turned around and nodded to one of his men, who grabbed her by her collar and dragged her out of the room. Lincoln was trying to load his weapon as Trent grabbed his hair and slammed his head down upon the desk.

"What the hell do you think you're doing? We have immunity." Lincoln cried out, but there was fear in his voice.

"Mr. Lincoln? Trent asked calmly

"You're a dead man, I'm telling you this, you are a dead man." Link screamed.

Trent ignored the threat, merely slamming his head against the table and repeating his question, "Mr. Lincoln?"

"Yes, yes, yes, I am Lincoln, what the hell do you want?"

"Tell me about Clarissa Maine."

***

"Are you seriously telling me that the House of Maine has made a direct attack on the Tallymen?" The Master's voice was filled with a mixture of anger and utter confusion as he stood up from behind his desk. "What is the problem? Aren't we paying off enough officials to ensure we are left alone?"

"It's not that, sir." The young guard stated. "It's Clarissa Maine. The Baron wants her back and has given his men orders to stop at nothing to ensure that happens. Somehow, they've discovered that she is now part of the Tallymen."

"Really? Well, that's certainly easy to rectify." The Master snorted. "We turn her over to them at once."

The guard frowned. "So have you not already made her part of the Tallymen?"

"I have, but these are extenuating circumstances. We only continue to function because we pay off the barons' people."

"But there is the code, sir." The guard stood aghast. "We stand by our people. We protect our people. We do not turn over our people to the authorities. This will not go down well with the sector chiefs."

The Master waved a dismissive hand. "Oh, I'm sure everyone will understand the situation. The code was never written for these circumstances."

"I'm not so sure, sir, but this is your order. I will get some of my men to bring Clarissa Maine in."

"It is so. Make sure it's done before the barons' men arrive in Regor."

"By your will, Sir."

# CHAPTER EIGHTEEN

# A Matter of Honour and Integrity

The tension in the house at 223 Sycamore Street was at its highest level. Kevin completely avoided Clarissa, and she couldn't help but feel frustrated at how she was now complicating her life even more. She'd never intended to kiss Richard; it just happened, and she was incredibly unsure of her feelings towards either man. She had always avoided romantic entanglements whenever possible. Indeed, the process of arranged marriage actively discouraged intimate relationships, at least for women.

She sat in front of the fire, sipping a nice cup of tea and pondering the events of the last couple of weeks. She pushed thoughts of the two men from her mind, focusing on what the future might hold. She had established herself within the Tallymen at the rank she would have liked, and little did she realise that authority her name would hold.

She was startled from her thoughts when there was a sharp rap at the front door. Once she realised what it was, she relaxed and went back to her thoughts while nursing her cup, leaving Maddie to deal with whoever was visiting. She didn't listen to the conversation between Maddie and the guest, at least not until their voices began to rise.

"I demand to see the Lady Clarissa." A gruff voice stated in a tone that made it clear it was in order. Clarissa immediately looked up in the direction of the voices, even though she could not see them from this position.

"Then I suggest you make an appointment," Maddie replied haughtily, but then there was a sudden gasp. "Take your hands off me at once." At these words, Clarissa was on her feet, pushing a lead ball into the barrel of her puffer and priming it.

Maddie came running in as the second lady of Jilrir raised her weapon, pointed it at the doorway, and was followed by two burly-looking men from the Tallymen. Clarissa had no evidence these were Tallymensmen, but even so...

The leader stopped and raised his hand slightly as he stared at the firearm. "I come from the Master of the Tallymen. Lower your weapon."

"I think not, Sir, for even the Master of the Tallymen has not the authority to walk into my residence unbidden. State your business and state it quickly."

"You are to come with me for a meeting with the Master," he replied

Clarissa narrowed her eyes. "Does the Master always send armed messengers to offer these invites?"

"When the need is urgent, yes, he does."

"Then go tell the Master that I will be by his office in due course."

"My orders are that you come with me. Don't make this difficult, Lady Clarissa."

"Oh my good Sir. It is you who are making this exceedingly difficult. You force your way in and continue to use my title despite the fact that the Master knows I'm supposed to be residing here in secret. You, I would guess, are no more than a humble Lieutenant and should not know who I am. So, either the Master is an idiot, or he sold me out, which is it?"

He flushed, looked at her awkwardly, and she became aware that it was the latter. "I see. The Tallymen's word is meaningless?" she sighed and fired her weapon, causing Maddie at her side to jump. The man stumbled back into his companion, who grabbed him and lowered him to the ground, keeping his eyes on the lady. She was slowly and carefully reloading her weapon, so he swiftly reached for a knife and stepped towards her, but Maddie swiftly moved to the table, grabbed up the teapot, and whacked it around his head. He was momentarily dazed, and when he focused once more, he was staring down the barrel of Clarissa's puffer. She fired.

Richard came running in and stopped, staring down at the two bodies on the floor. "Marran's beard, what the hell is going on now?"

"We have been betrayed, Richard, I believe the Tallymen has turned us in," said Clarissa as she stuffed her puffer back into her belt and stepped over the bodies.

"I will get us ready to leave at once." He sighed

Clarissa nodded, but as he turned her way, she gritted her teeth and said, "No. I want to find out exactly what the Tallymen has told our pursuers."

Richard stared back at her. "What exactly do you hope to achieve?"

"I'm not entirely sure, but wouldn't it at least be good to have a heads up on what is going on?"

"What if they just take you prisoner and turn you over?"

Clarissa gave a slight smirk. "Who said anything about going through the front door?" she said, and began reloading her weapon.

***

"You broke the code?" Gerard Bainbridge stared at the Master with a mixture of shock and contempt. The high-ranking member of the Tallymen was incredibly influential and could have been Master himself if he had been so inclined.

The Master looked up nervously. He knew his actions would be considered out of order, and Gerard Bainbridge could cause considerable trouble. "I had no choice, Gerard," he said determinedly. "You heard the report yourself. The House of Maine has decimated the Tallymen in Hayburn, and they will do the same here if we don't acquiesce to their demands."

"The code is what holds us together, you simpering idiot." Gerrard spat. "Our word is what holds us together. The Tallymen brings together all the rival syndicates, and for you to turn on Clarissa Maine means you can turn on any one of us."

"There won't be a Tallymen if the House of Maine destroys us," The Master protested.

"We can recover from whatever they do to us. We have done this before, but we cannot easily regain trust. The syndicates will break from the Tallymen and descend into a mob war." Gerard sighed.

"I would be hanged from the gates of the city," the Master said indignantly.

Gerard shook his head in disgust. "You odious slime, you are putting your own preservation above the needs of the Tallymen. I would challenge you to a Duel of Honor if it weren't for the consequences of doing so, and my business interests keep me far too busy for that."

"Then my position stands, Gerard. We will turn Clarissa Maine over to her family, and there's nothing you can do about it." The Master said firmly.

Gerard pondered for a moment. "We have one way. It is Clarissa Maine that you have dishonoured in this way; were we to propose a Duel of Honor between you and her, the Tallymen may be satisfied."

"You expect me to fight a Lady of Jilrir?" The Master looked appalled.

Gerard smiled. "If you kill her in a Duel of Honor, then the Tallymen will be sated, but she's hardly likely to accept the duel in the first place, and when she refuses, she will be branded as having accepted that your judgment is fair. We can't lose. This slip of a noble girl is hardly going to beat you, and she knows it. She won't accept."

***

"Where is Kevin?" Clarissa asked quietly as she and Richard headed down the steps of 223 Sycamore Street.

"We don't know, we think he's left."

Clarissa bit her lip. "You know what we did back there. You and me. It was a mistake. A spur-of-the-moment thing, and it should never have happened."

"Understood, my lady, but I think we have other concerns at hand," Richard said calmly as the pair headed down the street towards the headquarters of the Tallymen.

She had no idea of the chaos and panic that was going on since the news of Hayburn had arrived. However, she got an idea when she saw the typical guards who tried to look inconspicuous were not in the positions she had seen them in on a previous visit. Indeed, the fact that they could walk calmly through the front door, drawing their weapons, was most peculiar.

"Something is going on, my lady. I think we should withdraw to reconsider." Richard said uneasily, yet still primed his carbine.

"No, I want answers, and I'm not leaving without them," Clarissa responded determinedly.

"We may not be leaving at all if we're not careful," Richard muttered.

"I'm always careful, Richard." Clarissa smiled and winked at him.

"Now that's a perfect example of an oxymoron, my lady," Richard said, but he smiled back. The pair moved carefully through the lobby that was devoid of any signs of life. As they ventured further inside, they could hear raised voices shouting at each other, and whilst they could not make out what they were saying, they both felt sure they had heard the name Clarissa Maine coming from the Master's office. The door was slightly ajar, and Clarissa stopped at the entranceway, peering in the tiny gap to see the Master seated behind his desk and a white haired man she had never met before standing before it in a heated altercation.

Raising her weapon, he slowly pushed the door open as it ground on its hinges. The Master looked up, and the white-haired man spun round; both their eyes dropped to the firearm pointed at them.

"Speak of the bodragel here she is," the Master said softly, slowly rising to his feet.

"My Lady Clarissa," Gerard said, proffering her a slight bow. "It is an honor to meet you, but please lower your weapons. I give you my word, no one will harm you here."

"Oh, forgive me, gentlemen, maybe before the sun rose this morning, I would have accepted the word of a Tallymen member, but events have taken a different course." She kept the weapon primed and aimed. She did, however, take another step into the room, allowing Richard to follow her, his carbine ready.

"Yes indeed, the Master and I were currently discussing this predicament. I assure you, Lady Clarissa, I believe his actions are way out of line."

"And that may even mean something if I had any idea of who you are," Clarissa replied most politely.

"I am Gerard Bainbridge, master of the Southside Syndicate, the largest syndicate in Regor."

"Delighted to meet you, Master Bainbridge." Clarissa nodded to him. "If only it were in different circumstances. I'm here to find out what you have informed the agents of my family and then depart this city in haste."

"I ask that you delay that decision. The actions of the Master in betraying you have repercussions on many of the businesses throughout the land." Gerard stated. "You could potentially help save those and establish a place for you to remain in the city."

"I am listening." Clarissa narrowed her eyes.

"The Master has dishonoured you, and you have a right to demand satisfaction. In fact, it is expected of you."

"A Duel of Honor?" Richard snorted. "You expect this girl to fight with the Master? That is hardly a fair fight."

"No one asked Lady Clarissa to place herself in a position of the Tallymen." Gerard shrugged dismissively. "If she chooses to enter the man's world, then she has to abide by a man's rules. We are not giving her any exceptions."

"I will stand as second to the lady Clarissa!" Richard stepped forward determinedly.

"No, there are no seconds in a Tallymen Duel of Honor. Lady Clarissa either accepts the Duel of Honor, or she accepts the ruling of the Master."

"How about we simply shoot you where you stand," said Richard, raising his carbine.

"Kill the Master of the Tallymen? I suppose that is an option, but it will mean that you will have the Ravens pursuing you as well as your family, and your lady Clarissa.

"Well, we could just walk away," Clarissa said casually.

"And again we will be forced to hunt you, for we gave our word of honor to the House of Maine that we would turn you over, and we cannot break our word of honor twice in one day. Come on, Lady Clarissa, it's time to go home. No harm will come to you."

A silence hung in the air as Clarissa pondered this. Then, slowly lowering her weapons, she said, "I accept the duel."

The Master's mouth dropped open, and Gerard's eyes widened. At her side, Richard let out a weary sigh. "What happened to always being careful?" he muttered.

"It's not about me, Richard. He's right: should I go home, no substantial harm will come to me, although my life may become forever restricted. But my father will not let it pass that you and the others did what you did for me. Having the Tallymen also pursue us means it will go beyond the Province of Ithia, for the Tallymen has resources throughout the land. My father could continue to pursue me, but he does not have resources outside of his province."

Richard looked back at Gerard and the Master. "I think we should call their bluff. Whatever the nature of your death, the Baron will seek retribution."

"On the contrary." Gerrard smiled. "A Duel of Honor is a time-honoured tradition enshrined in law. Baron Maine will need to seek the king's approval for retribution, and given the considerable humiliation of the honourable Lady Clarissa, as caused to the crown, this is incredibly unlikely. However, I beseech you, my lady, to decline, for we are all aware that the Master will beat you."

"Indeed, that is probably the most likely outcome," Clarissa agreed. "But if I understand the duals of honor correctly, honor will be restored to me upon my death, and the Tallymen will be obligated to take care of those who are in my service. That you will need to protect my people from the retributions of the House of Maine, am I not correct?"

"You will sacrifice yourself for your people?" Gerard raised an eyebrow.

"My people put themselves in line for the hangman's noose the moment they decided to help me. I have personally led them to this situation, and I will honor my obligations to them. That is where the true honor lies, not in some foolish duel. That is no more than part of a political game you are now playing. Whilst the Master may win the duel, he will forever be the man who killed a woman whom he also betrayed. You may resolve your issue, but it won't be long before you replace the Master with someone who needs more credibility. But come now, this banter is pointless. I have accepted your terms; it's time to get this over with."

# CHAPTER NINETEEN

# *The Duel of Honor*

The small, unassuming warehouse on Buttercup Lane was not used for storage or any conventional business purposes. Euphemistically, it was referred to as 'The Arena' by members of the Tallymen. Its purpose was twofold: to offer trials by combat when someone was accused of breaking the code.

The Duel of Honor had a much higher standard, with repercussions that went far beyond proving innocence. Several hours after her meeting with Gerard and the Master, everything had been set up, the heads of the various syndicates had been summoned, a motley crew ranging from scruffy-looking thugs from the minor gangs up to official-looking businessmen in expensive garments, and bearing jewelry that was often garish and over the top.

Clarissa had Richard at her side, and Maddie and Taylor followed behind. All three had protested the stupidity of Clarissa's actions.

"I have no choice," Clarissa explained firmly. "Any alternative situation for me, but it won't resolve the situation for you. You have done much for me and sacrificed much for me, and should I die, the Tallymen will protect you from the House of Maine as a matter of their restored honor if you. I didn't make this decision lightly."

"No, but your death will make everything we have done pointless." Maddie had said, forcing back a tear. "Don't be so foolish, you petulant child."

Clarissa hugged her tightly. "Everything will be fine."

The assembled group stood in a circle with only a gap by the door for the competitors to enter. Guards stepped forward and put out their hands to prevent her companions from moving into the center with her. The Master was standing with Gerard at the other end in quite a cheerful mood.

He turned to look at Clarissa as she entered the circle, and she swallowed slightly as he smirked at her. Clarissa had proved herself to be no coward, but she knew this was going to hurt and hurt like hell. She looked back at her companions sadly. Kevin wasn't present, and she wondered where he had gone. She then looked up at the handsome Richard, pondering what could have been between either of those men. She had told him she was doing it for them, but there was another reason, one that was rooted in everything that she had done so far. She didn't want to go back to the House of Maine. Her new life was exciting and challenging, and whether she had married the Crown Prince or not, she would marry someone who would carry her on his arm as a trophy or political pawn, and end her days doing needlepoint, reading scripture, or attending functions as the submissive bride of some lord or other. No, she would indeed rather die, and dying this way would protect those whom she truly cared about.

All eyes were upon her, and there was a chattering murmuring around the hall. Some looked intrigued; others, appalled. As the Master stepped towards her, a tall, lanky gentleman dressed in fine robes finally stepped out of the assembled audience. "I protest. This cannot be an act of honor to beat down this small slip of a girl."

The Master did not reply, but Gerard spoke up. "As has been previously stated to the Lady Clarissa, if she ventures into the world of men, she will be treated like a man. She is subject to the rules of the Tallymen just like anyone else and has the opportunity to stand down and accept the judgment of the Master."

The tall man turned his gaze from Gerard back to the Master. He briefly glanced at Clarissa before saying, "Make it quick and make it painless."

Gerard stepped forward, standing just behind the Master and facing Clarissa. "Lady Clarissa Maine, you have called into question the honor and the integrity of the Master of the Tallymen in his recent actions. You have accepted a Duel of Honor, whereby the gods couldn't judge your actions."

At this, Taylor stepped forward and interrupted. "I say to you now, Illya does not judge this in your favor, Sir. Your actions are unjust, and she does not look favorably upon you."

"Ma'am, you are not a member of this Tallymen and here as a guest of Lady Clarissa." Gerard's voice rose. "If you cannot be silent, you will be removed."

"It's OK, sister, don't worry." Clarissa smiled at the priestess and hoped no one could hear the slight tremor in her voice.

"Here are the rules." Gerard continued. "One. The fight is to the death. Two. Both combatants will be unarmed. Three. They may not be aided by anyone in this room or out of it. Four. The combatants may utilize anything within the arena to aid them." Clarissa looked around the room and raised an eyebrow, but she saw there was literally nothing of use. The warehouse was barren and clearly deliberately so. "Let battle commence." And with that, he stepped back, and the

Master began to circle her with a huge grin that did indeed have its effect of intimidating her.

She backed away slightly and copied his movements as the two now circled each other. Clarissa didn't even see it coming when the Master leapt forward and slammed his fist into the side of her face. She flew back and down onto the ground, coming to rest on her backside and the palms of her hands. She was momentarily dazed, but saw his large leather boot coming towards her face. She rolled away just in time, jumping up to her feet as she spat blood from her mouth, but again his fist connected with her face. But she didn't lose her footing this time; she lashed out with a punch, but he merely pushed it away, bringing his other fist up into her stomach. She gagged and retched, allowing him time to bring his elbow down on her shoulder, and, knocking her down to her knees, she managed a punch to his stomach from this position. Still, he barely flinched, just taking a step back. Yet it enabled her to get back to her feet again. Once more, the fist pounded onto her face, knocking her back into the crowd. Someone grabbed her from behind and pushed her back into the center, staggering another punch impact to the side of her head, and she saw stars of vision blurred. However, she realized he wasn't intending to make it quick; her fumbling and flailing had given him ample opportunity to finish her off very quickly. No, he was making an example of her or exacting some form of vengeance. He intended to make her suffer. She needed to take advantage of this. They circled again, the grin still upon the man's face. She threw a punch. It struck him in the jaw, but again, there was little reaction other than a smirk. He threw out his hand and gripped around her throat, pulling her to him for the coup de grace. Instinctively, she grabbed at the hand, unable to breathe as he squeezed, struggling to free herself, as the light around her began to dim. With a sudden final move, she brought her bony knee up into his groin with all the force she could muster. The hand instantly released her and clutched his balls as he staggered back, bending over. She jumped forward, pushing his bald head down with all her might and throwing her weight over him to bring him to the ground, letting go as he fell from her reach.

Gasps went up from the crowd, and she was sure she heard Maddie shout out her name excitedly. She quickly brought her boot down on the side of his head. She stamped once more, but as he tried to get up, she swung a leg over his back and sat down upon him, riding him like a pony on his hands and knees. She reached her hands around his neck, but it was too large for her small fingers to get a grip. She needed something to wrap around it. She looked about, but there was nothing. Then it occurred to her... she reached up to the back of her neck and released the chain that supposedly symbolized the everlasting love between her and the crown prince. The Master rose to his hands and knees with her still on his back, trying not to fall off. Standing slightly, she dropped her weight so that he once more fell face down. She threw one end of the chain around his neck, and she pulled with all her might. It was his turn to scrabble at his neck, gasping for air. She rose and stood upon his back, continuing to pull until he gave up and stopped moving.

As Clarissa's body relaxed, she felt all the aches and pains of the strikes start to swell over her body. She spat out some blood on the back of the Master's head. The room was in total silence. Slowly, barely able to move, she turned around to face Gerard, who stood there, his eyes widened, his mouth agape.

"Well, that was..." he stopped looking for the right words. "Most unexpected."

"Is honor satisfied?" Clarissa said, barely able to speak through her swollen, split lip. Taylor quickly pushed her way through the group and came up to her side. She placed a hand on Clarissa's shoulder, but the young woman seemed not to notice that her eyes were fixed on Gerrard.

"I guess it is," Gerard replied, ignoring a couple of men who came forward to drag the body of the Master out of the arena.

"Wait a minute, Gerard, does this mean?..." A tall, well-dressed man stepped forward, his eyes filled with concern.

"I'm afraid it does." Gerard interrupted with a sigh as he stepped towards Clarissa. "Well played, my lady." To her surprise, he lowered himself to one knee and bowed his head. A chorus of shouts of disapproval went up around the room. Clarissa was so confused and looked around the room. "Silence. The code is clear." Gerard shouted. "Bend the knee." There was hesitation, then, slowly, a few of the assembled crowd began to lower themselves, and others followed suit until only Clarissa's companions remained standing, looking just as confused as she.

Light blue sparkles began to travel around Clarissa's body as the priestess standing behind her, her hand still on her shoulder, started to mutter a prayer. With bowed heads, few saw, but those who did stifled gasps as her swollen face started to move into something more normal.

Clarissa looked down at Gerard. "Well, OK, what is going on?"

"The Code is quite clear. Defeat of the Master in a Duel of Honour means the victor is now the head of the Tallymen."

"If I may be permitted to speak," said the young man. "She is a woman."

"Our code does not dictate that the leader has to be a man; it wasn't thought as necessary. But she can decline the position." Gerard raised his head and looked at her hopefully.

There was a long silence as Clarissa stared down at him, her mind racing with all the implications of what he was saying, but a smile crossed her now perfect lips. "Oh no, good, Sir, I accept. And can I add now ask, but in my new position, it is the Talleymen's responsibility to ensure my safety."

Gerard's final hope was gone, and he said weakly, "That is the case, my lady."

She looked back at her companions and squeezed Taylor's hand, indicating thanks for the healing. The rest of her group was standing, staring. She chuckled lightly before turning back to Gerard. "Well, then, my good Sir, we will have a surprise waiting for Master Seargeant Trent. It would appear the Tallymen are now at war with the House of Maine."

Clarissa Maine returns in The Usurper of Jilrir.

***Perceptions***

Jenna Plural Wants You – Michael Phelkar

That Girl from Wagga – Stacey Grant

Walking in Her Shadow - Emma Dodgson

Awakening of Hannah Grant – Hannah Grant

The Angel of Phobos – Bridgette Toussaint

Memoir of a Martian – Kyla Lieberman

The Rings of Venus – Liam Marshall

Day of the GenMods – Tabitha

*The Kensett Files*

*(A Perceptions Series)*

Out of the Darkness

The Hand of Jenna

***The Cult of Artemis Baily***

The Rise of Artemis: The Golden Age Edition

***The Amazon Chronicles***

Miss Eve and the City of Men

***The House of Maine***

The House of Maine

Escape from Jilrir

Rise of the Shieldmaidens

Blood of the Esselar

THE HOUSE OF MAINE
DAVID PARKER ROSS

PERCEPTIONS
Jenna Plural
Wants You
PERCEPTIONS
PERCEPTIONS
Walking in
Her Shadow
PERCEPTIONS
PERCEPTIONS
The Angel
Of Phobos
Memoir of
a Martian
PERCEPTIONS
The Rings
of Venus
PERCEPTIONS
PERCEPTIONS
It's All About Who You Believe

www.ingramcontent.com/pod-product-compliance
Lightning Source LLC
LaVergne TN
LVHW091054080826
845145LV00002B/738